Joseph Anton Keller

Saint Anthony

ancedotes proving the miraculous power of St. Anthony

Joseph Anton Keller

Saint Anthony
ancedotes proving the miraculous power of St. Anthony

ISBN/EAN: 9783337335717

Printed in Europe, USA, Canada, Australia, Japan

Cover: Foto ©Andreas Hilbeck / pixelio.de

More available books at **www.hansebooks.com**

PREFACE.

PERHAPS no saint, after our blessed Lady and St. Joseph, is more popular and venerated than the great St. Anthony of Padua.

Although in many lands, owing to revolution and persecution, the Franciscan churches where the devotion to this great saint first began have been destroyed, it still remains as flourishing as ever, and every year thousands in all parts of the world make the nine Tuesdays in his honor.

It cannot, therefore, be doubted that the following anecdotes, derived from reliable sources, will not only interest the devout clients of St. Anthony, but will also strengthen and encourage them to still greater confidence in his powerful intercession.

3

CONTENTS.

—

PART II. MIRACLES WORKED AFTER THE
DEATH OF ST. ANTHONY.

PAGE.

Part III. Petitions Granted in More Modern Times.

PAGE.

PART I.

MIRACLES WORKED DURING THE LIFE OF ST. ANTHONY.

1.—The Miracle of Tongues.

A MONG the saints of the Church few are better known than the great St. Anthony of Padua.

Endowed with great natural gifts, enjoying excellent health, a powerful voice, combined with great eloquence, an admirable delivery, a perfect knowledge of the Scriptures and theology, he was, soon after his ordination, sent to preach in France, Italy and Portugal.

Although in his youth he had never spoken anything but Portuguese, he, like the apostles after Pentecost, received that wonderful gift of tongues, which not only enabled him to preach even with eloquence in French and Italian, but to make himself understood by people from all parts of the world.

An instance of this may be given: When ordered by the Holy See to preach the Lenten sermons at Rome he was perfectly understood by the immense multitude from all nations, whom the renown of his great sanctity and marvellous gifts had attracted. This same gift was of most frequent occurrence during his missionary career.

2.—Dumb Animals Obey the Saint.

There was near the monastery of the Friars Minor, at Montpellier, a large pool filled with frogs, whose perpetual croakings greatly disturbed the saint and his community. At last, wearied by this perpetual noise, he determined to put an end to it, and going to the pond, after blessing it, ordered the frogs to stop their croaking, which at once ceased, and the pond from that time was called St. Anthony's Pond.

But stranger still, if a frog was taken out of this pond and placed in another, it instantly recovered its power of croaking, while it was just the reverse were a strange frog put into St. Anthony's Pond.

3.—The Sermon to the Fishes at Rimini.

During the eleventh and twelfth centuries Europe had much to suffer from various heresies, more especially from that of the Albigenses, which infested the south of France and north of Italy.

God, ever watchful over His spouse,
the Church, soon raised up two great
men, St. Francis and St. Dominic,
who, with their sons, came to her assistance.

St. Anthony of Padua, on account
of his great sanctity and learning, was
chosen by his superiors to be one of
the first to enter the battlefield. Rimini, in Romagna, in spite of all the
endeavors of the Holy See and of its
own saintly bishop, continued to remain the hotbed of heresy, and here
it was St. Anthony began his arduous
task of conversion.

The heretics, on hearing who was
to enter the lists against them, were
filled with dismay, but instigated by
the evil one, resolved at any cost to
face their enemy.

The saint on his arrival met with
the reverse of a cordial reception; the

church in which he was to begin his labors was empty, save for a few old men and women; but his longing for the glory of God and salvation of souls was too great to make him hesitate for a moment. He therefore ascended the pulpit, and preached with such earnestness and zeal that the heretics, on hearing about it, determined to leave nothing undone to get rid of one who was so dangerous an opponent.

This great servant of God, being informed of their intentions, withdrew to a remote part of the city, to prepare himself by prayer, fasting and penance for the encounter, imploring at the same time the mercy of God on this poor benighted people.

His enemies had, however, not lost sight of him, and on seeing him leave his retreat, some of them followed him to the place where the river Marecchia empties itself into the Adriatic. Here the saint stopped, and in a loud voice commanded the fishes of the sea and river to come forth and listen to the word of God, saying: "Come, ye senseless fishes of the deep, and by your attention to the word of your God and mine, put to shame these men, who in their blindness and hardness of heart refuse to hear it."

The words were barely out of the saint's mouth before a great commotion was noticed in the sea. Thousands of fishes of every size and species were seen to come in the greatest order to its surface, the smaller ones placing themselves in front, and the larger ones behind. Then began one of the most extraordinary sermons ever preached. The saint addressed them as if they were beings endowed with reason.

"Oh! ye fishes of the deep, praise and thank your God and Creator for the unspeakable blessings He has lavished on you, favoring you above all dumb animals. See and admire the beautiful home He, in His infinite goodness, has prepared for you; look at those crystal waters, in which it is so easy for you to find a refuge against the storm and the enemy. Not only has He provided for all your wants, but He has made you prolific above all other creatures. You alone have been exempted from the dominion of your fellow beings and from His wrath at the time of the deluge. To you it has been given to save His prophet Jonas; to cure His blind servant Tobias; to be the food of the penitent; to procure for the Saviour of

mankind and His disciples the tribute
money due to Cæsar; it was after His
Resurrection by eating of your flesh
He proved He was truly risen from
the dead; it was over your heads He
walked on the sea, and after the great
draught of fishes, He called His apostles 'fishers of men.' "

The fishes seemed to be filled with
admiration, and anxious not to lose
one of his words, their numbers ever
increasing, marking their approval
by the lifting up and down of their
heads, the opening of their mouths,
but not one of them thought of leaving
the spot till the saint had blessed them,
and ordered them to return to their
homes below, when they immediately
disappeared. But the commotion of
the waters continued for some time
after. In the meantime, so deep had
been the impression made upon the

bystanders, eye-witnesses of this re-
markable scene, that many hastened
back to the city, imploring their
friends to come and see the miracle;
others burst into tears, and kneeling
at the feet of the saint, implored forgiveness, while only a few remained
obdurate in their heresy.

St. Anthony, availing himself of this
opportunity, at the close of the sermon to the fishes addressed the immense multitude now gathered together, exhorting them to repentance,
rebuking them for their unbelief and
ingratitude, pointing out to them the
heinousness of sin, and showing them
what a lesson of obedience the fishes
had just given them.

It was through this sermon that
Rimini was purged from heresy.

4.—Why St. Anthony is Invoked for Lost and Mislaid Things.

The following incident in the life of St. Anthony accounts for his being invoked for lost and mislaid articles:

During his stay at the Franciscan monastery at Montpellier St. Anthony was not only engaged in preaching, but also in teaching theology to his younger brethren. It was here a most extraordinary adventure happened to one of his novices. The latter, weary of the monastic life, suddenly left the monastery, taking with him a book of psalms, copied and annotated by the saint for the benefit of his pupils.

The loss of this book was deeply felt by St. Anthony, as books at that time were only written, the art of printing being unknown, an ordinary book costing at least a hundred dollars of our money.

In the year 1240 the monks at Camaldoli paid as much as two hundred gold ducats for an illuminated missal. (See History of Pope Innocent III.. volume iv.) Whole fortunes sometimes were spent in the purchase of a single book.

What pained the saint even more than the loss of a work invaluable to him, was the outrage committed against God, and the spiritual danger threatening the culprit. The saint, with his usual trust in God, at once betook himself to prayer, humbly imploring the divine mercy on the unhappy youth, and at the same time asking for the restitution of his book. His prayer was barely finished before it was heard. Just at that moment, as the thief was about to cross a bridge, the devil, in the shape of a hideous negro, appeared before him with an axe in his hand, threatening at once to kill him and trample him under foot if he did not immediately retrace his steps. The novice, terrified at the sight of the monster, hastened to obey, and falling at the feet of the servant of God, not only gave back the book, but implored forgiveness, begging to be readmitted into the monastery.

The saint, full of gratitude to God, readily forgave the culprit, warning him at the same time against the snares of the devil and encouraging him to persevere in his holy vocation. The stolen book has been for years preserved in the Franciscan monastery at Bologna.

5.—A Messenger from Hell Unmasked.

While the saint was preaching at Puy a messenger suddenly appeared in the midst of the congregation, calling out to a lady in a loud voice that her son had been foully murdered by his enemies. Anthony, who easily discovered who the messenger was, commanded silence by a motion of his hand, and, after consoling the lady by telling her that her son was never in better health in his life and that she would shortly see him, added that the supposed messenger was no other than the evil one, who had only come in the hopes of disturbing the sermon and marring its effects. This proved perfectly true, as the pretended messenger at once vanished. The saintly preacher then availed himself of the opportunity thus presented to him to warn his hearers against the artifices of the evil one.

6.—The Consoler of Mothers.

Whilst at Brives God glorified His servant by making him work many miracles.

A poor woman had gone to hear the saint preach, leaving her child alone, with no one to take care of him. During her absence the little one fell into a caldron of boiling water, and on her return she found him playing unhurt in his dangerous bath.

But a greater miracle than that was worked on another occasion. A mother having left her infant at home by itself, in order to go and hear the sermon, found him on her return dead in his cradle. In the midst of her grief she rushed back to the church and informed the saint of what had taken place. "Go home," he replied, "your son liveth," making use of the same words as Our Lord did when the father asked Him to cure his son. Full of confidence in St. Anthony, she hastened back, and to her great joy, found the baby up and playing with his little companions.

7.—The Rain Respects the Friend of the Saints.

It happened one day that the cook of the monastery at which the saint was staying had nothing to give the brethren to eat, and went and told Anthony of his difficulty. The saint at once went to see a pious lady he knew, begging her to have compassion on his brethren and send them a few cabbages. So great was the veneration

in which he was held that she immediately, in spite of the inclemency of
the weather, for it was pouring
rain, ordered her servant to go into
the garden and cut as many vegetables
as the monks would require.   The
maid obeyed and took them to the
convent. Notwithstanding the drench-
ing rain, she returned home perfectly
dry, and, full of admiration, said to her
mistress: "When you want something
done for Father Anthony or the other
monks, do, pray, send me; I would
not care if the weather was a thousand
times worse than to-day; see, there is
not a drop of rain on my clothes and
my shoes are not even damp."

The lady, full of admiration, earnestly recommended the monks to the
care of her only brother, a canon at
Noblet, entreating him to assist them,
as far as lay in his power, and to rest

assured that God would reward him a hundredfold for his charity.

8.—An Extraordinary Prophecy.

While the saint was at his monastery at Puy he used sometimes to meet a lawyer, who led a very bad and profligate life. Every time they met the saint would uncover his head and bow most respectfully to him. Thinking the servant of God was only laughing at him, the lawyer one day turned round and said to him: "If I did not fear the judgment of God I would soon make you repent of insulting one who has never injured you, by thrusting my sword through your body." The saint replied that, far from having any intention of insulting him, he only bowed through a feeling of deep love and respect, for in thus saluting him he was saluting one who was to be a glorious martyr, and begged of him, when undergoing his tortures, not to forget him in his prayers. The lawyer for the time being laughed at what seemed to him to be a most unlikely thing. Strange to say, the prophecy was shortly afterwards fulfilled. A bishop started for Palestine, with the intention of converting the Saracens, and urged on by a secret impulse from heaven, the lawyer followed him. On his arrival he was suddenly filled with such a desire to convert the infidels that he himself at once began to preach the truths of the Christian religion to them and point out the wickedness of Mahometanism, which so enraged these fanatics that after making him a prisoner and torturing him for three days, they put him to death. When about to die he revealed to those present how the saintly

Father Anthony had predicted his martyrdom, declaring at the same time that a great prophet had risen in their midst.

9.—St. Antbony tbe Consoler of Persecuted Women.

St. Anthony always took a great interest in women in distress, or persecuted, and they therefore look on him as their special protector.

Among those who, owing to the sanctity of the Franciscans, held them in great veneration and aided them in their daily wants, was a lady who suffered much from a jealous and irritable husband. One evening, after finishing some work and making some purchases for the Brothers, finding it too late to take them to the monastery that night, she took them home with her. This so greatly roused the anger and jealousy of her husband that, not content with loading her with re-proaches, he pulled almost all her hair off her head. The poor woman was naturally greatly hurt at such treatment, but full of confidence in her good Father Anthony, after carefully gathering up all her hair, she wrote, begging of him to call on her the next day. Her trust in the saint was not misplaced. After hearing her story he immediately on his return to his monastery, summoned his community together and begged of them to unite with him in praying for their bene-factress. These prayers were not in vain, for before they were finished the pain left her and her head was covered with hair, as if nothing had happened. The sight of this miracle was not only the means of converting her husband,

but also of making him a great benefactor to the monastery.

10.—Truth from the Lips of a Little Child.

St. Anthony, when travelling
through Romagna, not only visited
Padua, but also Polesine and Ferrara.
He remained some time in the last
place and worked a miracle as touch-
ing in its circumstances as it was bene-
ficial in its results. A nobleman in
that city had married a lady of remark-
able beauty and highly gifted. Her
rare talents, winning manners and ac-
complishments soon made her a general favorite in society, which so in-
censed her husband and excited his
jealousy that it was hardly possible for
her to live with him, and their home
became one scene of continual strife.

The birth of a lovely boy, far from

bringing peace to the unhappy couple,
only increased the suspicions of the
wretched father, who now, under the
complete power of the evil one, determined to destroy both mother and
child. Whilst he was thus fostering
these evil thoughts in his mind, St.
Anthony came to preach a mission in
this city, and the lady, like Susanna of
old, came to this new Daniel, certain
that she would through his intercession obtain the conversion of her husband.

What follows will show how success
attended the prayers of the servant of
God. Not long afterward, whilst this
gentleman and several others were
talking together with the saint on the
public square, the mother, as if inspired by God, sent the nurse to take a
walk with the infant. At the sight of
the child the jealous husband bit his

lips with vexation and anger. St. Anthony, on the contrary, drew near the nurse and began caressing the child, asking him, as if in a joke, "Who is your father, my little one?" The bystanders smiled at this childish question. But the servant of God had an object in view, the justification of the innocent. The little babe, only a few weeks old, smilingly turning his face to where his father stood, replied in a clear voice, to the astonishment of all present: "There is my father." St. Anthony, putting the child into the arms of the now delighted parent, said: "Take the child and never again doubt he is your son, since he himself has told you so." The happy husband at once carried him home in triumph to his mother, and from that time peace and joy reigned in this favored household.

The news of this event spread far and wide, and there is a memento of it to be seen sculptured in marble in the chapel of the saint at Padua.

11.—Broken Goblet and Running Barrel.

The Vicar-General of the Franciscan Order, Brother Elias, on the death of the saintly founder, St. Francis of Assisi, in a pathetic circular convoked all the superiors of the various provinces to attend a general chapter, in order to proceed to the election of his successor. It was probably in the autumn of A. D. 1226 that Anthony, accompanied by one of his brethren, went to Italy, passing through Provence in order to be present at this general chapter.

On their way through Provence they stopped to rest at one of the

towns, in the house of a pious woman.
She, being anxious to pay her weary
guests as much respect as she possibly
could, borrowed a splendid cut glass
goblet from one of her neighbors for
them to drink their wine out of. Unfortunately the companion of the saint,
wanting to examine it more closely,
took it up in his hand and broke it.
This was not the only mishap. The
kind hostess, thinking only of the comfort of her guests, forgot to turn the
tap of the barrel when she went to
draw their wine, and on returning to
the cellar found it had all run out. The
saint, seeing how distressed she was
by these misadventures, bowed his
head in prayer, and to the great astonishment of the good woman, who
was silently watching him, she saw the
broken pieces of the goblet unite together, leaving no mark of breakage.

Full of hope, she ran to the cellar, and to her great joy, the barrel, which before the occurrence was half empty, was now filled with the most delicious wine.

St. Anthony, in his deep humility, at once continued his journey to Italy, so as to avoid the applause awaiting him as soon as the news of this fresh miracle got abroad.

12.—The Carved Capon.

St. Anthony was one day invited by a party of heretics to come to dine with them, in order, as they said, to give them the opportunity of laughing at his stupidity. He good-naturedly accepted their invitation. After sitting down to table a large bat, such as are found in Sicily, was served up to him, with the request to carve it. When, without being the least disconcerted,

he began to do so, they could hardly
refrain from laughing aloud; but soon
their laughter was changed into astonishment, for hardly had the saint
begun to carve the wretched bird before it was changed into a magnificent
capon, emitting the most delicious
smell. This miracle so completely
changed their hearts that they not only
acknowledged the power of the servant of God, but renounced their
errors and were received into the
Church.

13.—Tbe Apparition of tbe Iboly Cbilo.

The Friars Minor had no monastery
within the walls of Padua, the nearest
one, at Arcella, outside the city, being
about three-quarters of an hour's
walk. It often happened that, owing
to the gates being closed early in the
evening, it was impossible for the

saint on account of his missionary
work, to return home. But he easily
found a night's shelter among his
friends, who were only too happy to
have him for their guest. Tito Bor-
ghese, Count of Campo San Pietro, one
of the saint's dearest friends, was
among the few whom he honored the
most with his presence. This nobleman had so great a veneration for him
that he carefully noted down all that
took place during his visits, even ris-
ing up at night to watch his guest
through the keyhole. Once, when
thus visiting him, he noticed an extraordinary light piercing through the
chinks of the saint's apartments. Anxious to discover the cause of this, he
drew near, and to his great surprise
saw through the cracks of the door St.
Anthony holding a beautiful child in
his arms, whom he was lovingly

caressing. His host was first at a loss
to understand how this lovely infant
had entered the apartment of his
guest, but soon discovered, through
his majestic bearing and the rapture of
S.. Anthony, that the child was no
other than our divine Lord, who, under this form, had come to console,
encourage and strengthen His faithful
servant. The apparition lasted some
time, then suddenly disappeared, leaving the room in total darkness. At
once the saint rose from his prayers,
and on going to his bedroom,
knocked against his host in the dark.
As if guilty of a crime, he entreated
his friend not to betray his secret.
During the lifetime of St. Anthony the
Count faithfully kept his word, but
after his death, with tears streaming
down his face, he gave a minute account of everything that had taken

place. The heavenly light, of a bluish color, issuing forth from the divine Child, although brighter and more beautiful than the sun, did not dazzle the eye, whilst at the same time the heart was filled with unutterable joy. He, moreover, declared that the holy Child Himself had informed the saint, by pointing to the door with His finger, that he was watched, but that St. Anthony appeared to pay no attention to this, as if anxious not to deprive his friend of this heavenly consolation. He furthermore added that the holy Child was standing on the breviary of the saint.

This apparition has been so frequently mentioned by old historians that its veracity cannot be doubted. It is for this reason St. Anthony is usually represented with the holy Child standing on his breviary.

14.—Flight to Lisbon.

While the father of St. Anthony, Don Martin de Buglione, was living at Lisbon a murder was committed in the street close to his house and the corpse thrown into his garden, so that suspicion might fall upon him. The nobleman was in fact accused of the murder, thrust into prison, and a long and painful trial began, with every prospect of ending in his being condemned to death. St. Anthony was just then at the monastery in Padua working for the interests of that God for whose sake he had left everything dear to him. But God, in permitting this accusation, intended through it to make His beloved child known and glorified in his own land. Informed during prayer of his father's situation, he, in spite of his being provincial, went at once, according to his usual custom, to beg permission from the superiors to absent himself from the monastery for a few days. This granted, he started for Lisbon, convinced he would reach that city before sentence of death had been pronounced, meanwhile continuing his prayers for his unhappy parent. After journeying some distance he suddenly found himself transported to Lisbon, and his feelings can be easily imagined on re ceiving this fresh favor from heaven He at once went to the place where the court was sitting. and began to plead his poor father's cause. The judges, although struck by the eloquence and cleverness of this strange Father, could not be convinced of the innocence of the accused. Anthony, repulsed by men, did not lose heart, and after a few moments spent in prayer, without asking leave or giving the judges time to recover from their astonishment, went to the cemetery, followed by the judges and an immense crowd of people, attracted hither by curiosity, and ordered the body of the murdered man to be exhumed. As soon as the coffin was visible he then, in a loud voice, in the name of God, commanded the deceased to bear witness before the judges present as to whether Don Martin de Buglione was his murderer or not. The corpse at once obeyed, and sitting up, one hand raised and the other leaning against the ground, replied in a clear and sonorous voice: "Don Martin de Buglione is not my murderer." The youth then entreated St. Anthony to give him the priestly absolution from excommunication which his sudden death had deprived him of. After receiving it he quietly laid himself down in his coffin, not to be disturbed again. As for St. Anthony, he suddenly disappeared from both judges and people, who cried aloud, as if awaking from a dream: "A miracle! a miracle! a great miracle!" It was thus that through the intervention of his son Don Martin de Buglione was declared innocent and restored to liberty.

The reply, "I am come to save the innocent, and not to betray the guilty," which St. Anthony made to the judges when asked who was then the real culprit, soon spread far and wide. He returned back to the monastery of Santa Maria dell'Arcella in the same miraculous manner after an absence of one day and two nights.

15.—St. Anthony again Rescues His Father.

St. Anthony's father held an important post at the court of Lisbon. What it was is not exactly known; but it is certain he had a great deal to do in the management of the royal revenues. Owing to the fact that he always thought others as good and honest as himself, he one day neglected asking for a receipt from certain officials of the royal household, to whom he had paid large sums of money. The latter, jealous of his high position, and more especially of the royal favors lavished on him, had long been waiting for an opportunity to ruin him. They, therefore, gladly availed themselves of this occasion, declaring they had not received the money. A lawsuit was begun, and he certainly must have lost it for want of proofs but for the intervention of his son, Anthony, who suddenly appeared before the dishonest officials, and, looking them straight in the face, bore witness as to the day, hour, place, and even coin, in which the money had been paid, at the same time threatening them with the vengeance of God did they not at once give the required receipt. Terrified at having to confront such a witness, the enemies of the count acknowledged having received the money, and from that time Don Martin de Buglione was no longer molested by his enemies.

16.—Where Thy Treasure is, There also is Thy Heart.

Among the many vices infesting Florence, usury was the one against which the saint waged the greatest war.

St. Bonaventure himself relates an occurrence which took place in that city, and of which St. Anthony availed himself in one of his sermons to illustrate how severely God punishes that vice.

A rich usurer died, and whilst the saint was in prayer God revealed to him that this man's soul was in hell on account of his unjust dealings with others. An immense crowd of people had gone to hear the saint preach the funeral sermon. He at once, on ascending the pulpit, began by pointing out the heinousness of the sin of usury, declaring that usurers in their thirst for gold were the enemies of mankind, desiring nothing so much as war, famine, pestilence and so forth, so as to enrich themselves at the expense of

others, and satisfy their craving for
those riches in which their happiness
alone consisted. Then, speaking with
still greater emphasis, he exclaimed:
"They are also the enemies of their
own souls, for it is indeed rare for a
usurer to become holy." Adding:
"This is precisely what has happened
to the one to whom these last honors
are being paid," and pointing to the
catafalque before him, he continued:
"To prove the truth of my assertion
you need only go and look at the
chest of money, which, for the short
time he lived on earth, was the joy and
god of his heart, and you will find
there that heart lying under his gold.
For the Son of God Himself has declared, 'Where thy treasure is there
also is thy heart.'"

The people at this announcement
remained at first perfectly dumbfound-

ed, after which crowds of them rushed
to the house of the deceased in order
to ascertain for themselves the truth
of this assertion, insisting upon the
chest being opened, and there, to their
great astonishment, found the heart
still warm, lying under the gold. But
not yet fully convinced of the truth,
they again returned to the church
where the corpse was lying, and on
opening the body found no heart in it.
Filled with indignation against the
usurer, they declared his body should
not be buried in consecrated ground,
and taking it off the catafalque,
dragged it out of the city and threw it
on a place where dead beasts were
buried.

This wonderful occurrence did not
fail to produce a good and lasting impression on the people. From that
time usury was almost stamped out of

Florence; but the respect and veneration in which St. Anthony was held
were such that he and his companion
fled from the city to seek the solitude
of Mt. Alvernia.

17.—St. Anthony Cures a Cripple.

Whilst the saint was at Padua a
youth called Leonardo accused himself in confession of having kicked his
mother so violently that she fell to the
ground. St. Anthony, wishing to
make him understand the enormity of
his crime, said to him: "The foot of
one who kicks father or mother de-
serves to be cut off." The young man
did not understand his words in the
sense he meant them, and on returning home actually went and chopped
off the foot with which he had kicked
his mother. This news soon reached

the ears of the saint, who at once went to see the youth. After making the sign of the cross upon the mutilated limb both leg and foot were again joined together, without leaving any mark.

18.—Bilocation of the Saint.

Another wonderful miracle has been handed down to posterity. Whilst preaching on Easter Sunday in the cathedral at Montpellier the saint suddenly remembered he had to sing the Alleluia at the convent Mass. He paused for an instant and was silent, as if trying to get breath. But in reality he was singing the Alleluia in his own monastery, after which he resumed his sermon. Such occurrences naturally caused St. Anthony to be held in great veneration by everybody.

19.—Wind and Rain Obey St. Anthony.

Another extraordinary occurrence took place at Bourges, in France, the representation of which was long to be seen carved on one of the portals of the cathedral.

Owing to the vast crowds who wanted to hear the saint preach, it was found impossible for any of the churches or squares within the city to contain them. It was therefore decided to hire a large field outside the city walls, and the people, headed by the canons and clergy, walked in procession to the place. Fortunately it was summer. When St. Anthony began his first sermon the weather was magnificent, but suddenly the sky became overcast, a high wind began to blow, dark clouds were seen floating in the air, and distant peals of thunder

were heard. The immense crowd became alarmed and began to think of
seeking shelter, when the saint, noticing the movement, quietly said to
them: "Do not be frightened, remain
in your places; not one drop of rain will
touch you." Full of confidence in his
words not one left, and St. Anthony
continued his sermon in the midst of
a most terrific hail and thunder-storm,
and neither the saint nor his vast congregation received one drop of rain.
Even the ground on which they stood
was perfectly dry, just in the same
manner as when ages before the Israel-
ites passed through the waters of the
Red Sea.

At the sight of the miracle a hymn
of praise and thanksgiving to that
God whom the rain and winds obey
burst forth from the lips of all those
present, who were also filled with still

greater respect and veneration toward
one whom God so highly favored.

20.—Zeal for the Word of God.

The more St. Anthony endeavored
to remain hidden and unknown, the
more did God exalt His servant before his death. A noble lady, richly
dressed, was going to hear one of the
Lenten sermons preached by the saint,
accompanied by her servants. Absorbed in her own thoughts, she paid
little attention to the road, and fell into
a pool filled with dirty water. She naturally expected to be covered with
mud, which, to her great vexation,
would have prevented her from hearing the sermon. Strange to say, on
her being assisted out of the pool, not
a speck of mud was to be seen on her
clothes.

The news of this miracle was soon

repeated from mouth to mouth, and was universally attributed to the prayers of St. Anthony.

A twofold lesson can be learned from it. First, that extravagance in dress, even in the wealthy, is displeasing to God, and secondly, that the hearing of the word of God is certain to bring down a blessing.

21.—The Saint's Sermon is heard at a Great Distance.

A woman, living at about an hour's distance from the church where the saint was to preach, wanted very much to hear him, but was prevented, owing to her husband's illness. Not able to console herself for the loss, she stepped out on to the balcony and leaning on the railings, longingly looked in the direction where the sermon was being preached. Suddenly she fancied

she could hear every word the preacher said, as distinctly as if she had been
inside the church. Fearing it might
be an illusion, she ran and begged her
husband to come and listen. The sick
man at once complied with her request, and he also distinctly heard
what the saint said. Their joy can be
easily imagined; but in order to be
sure it was no illusion on their part,
they asked their neighbors on their
coming home what was the subject of
the sermon, and then informed them of
what had taken place, to the greater
glory of God and of His holy servant
Anthony.

22.—Cure of a Paralyzed Child.

One day after his sermon, as the saint
was hurrying back to his monastery,
in order to avoid the applause of the

multitude, he was stopped by a man carrying in his arms a little girl, both of whose feet were paralyzed, so that it was impossible for her to walk. Besides this, she suffered from epileptic fits of extraordinary violence. The unhappy father, full of confidence in the saint, determined to ask his assistance, and kneeling at his feet, holding the little one in his arms, implored him to bless her. Filled with pity for the unhappy parent, St. Anthony immediately did as requested. On his return home the poor man, certain his child was cured, placed her on the ground, making her stand, holding by the rail of a bench. Shortly afterward, when she began to take a few steps, he gave her a stick, but soon that was discarded, and Padovana, full of glee, was seen running about the room, perfectly cured. From that time she never suffered either from epilepsy or paralysis.

These wonderful cures were almost of daily occurrence, so that the same thing could have been said of the saint as of Our Lord: "He went about doing good and curing all."

23.—A Martyr's Death Predicted.

God also bestowed upon His servant the gift of prophecy, and the saint predicted to a woman at Assisi that the son about to be born to her would suffer martyrdom, which indeed happened. He was called Philip, and after joining the Franciscans was sent to Asia, recently recaptured from the Christians by the Saracens. After courageously refusing to abjure Christianity and embrace Mahometanism, he was cruelly tortured, being flayed alive, and he, with several other Christians whom he encouraged to suffer martyrdom, was beheaded.

24.—Death of St. Anthony.—The Great Miracle Worked after his Death.

The city of Padua, so often the scene of St. Anthony's apostolic labors during his lifetime, was also to witness his death. On his return to that city, just before Lent, he was entreated to preach the Lenten sermons. This, in spite of his excessive weakness, he agreed to do. But hardly were they finished before he felt himself attacked with that illness which he knew would be his last. He received all the sacraments with the greatest devotion, having only one desire left, that of soon beholding the face of his God.

On the 13th of June, whilst the saint

was lying in his death agony on his wretched pallet, in a small convent near Padua, towards evening the news reached the city that he was ill, dying.

Immediately an immense crowd of people hastened to the monastery to ascertain the truth, and receive a last blessing from their beloved father. When about to breathe his last the dying saint, as if anxious to give one more token of his love for our blessed Lady, was distinctly heard, in the midst of the tears and sobs of those surrounding his bedside, to sing in an angelic voice the beautiful line: *O gloriosa Domina, excelsa super sidera*— "O glorious Mother of God, raised above the skies," and with these words on his lips he expired.

God, to glorify His saint, worked many miracles in his behalf, but the greatest took place A. D. 1326, thirty-two years after his death. The inhabitants of Padua had built a magnificent church in his memory, and St. Bonaventure came himself to superintend the removal of the body. On opening the coffin nothing but bones were found, except the tongue, which was exactly the same as when the saint was alive. At this sight St. Bonaventure, falling on his knees, thus apostrophized it: "O blessed tongue, who hast so often praised thy God, now does He, in His turn, make manifest how great are thy merits." He then placed it in a magnificent casket, covered with precious stones, and carried it to the chapel, where it is still to be seen.

PART II.

MIRACLES WORKED AFTER THE DEATH OF ST. ANTHONY.

25.—A Skull Injured.

A YOUNG relative of the saint had so injured his skull through a fall that there was no hope of saving him through human means. The child was taken and placed on the altar dedicated to St. Anthony, and was so completely cured that he never suffered from any pain in his head again.

26.—The Picture of St. Anthony.

In the year 1683, Antonia Palormi, a young girl of fourteen, living at Naples, fell on her head from a great

height on to the top of a stone building. She bled profusely from her right
ear and was half killed. The child,
who had a great devotion to her name-
sake, St. Anthony, not only wore a
picture of the saint round her neck,
but used daily to recite the thirteen
Our Fathers and Hail Marys in his
honor. In the midst of her battle between life and death, he appeared to
her, and taking hold of her by her
hair, said: "Even had you not called
upon me, I would have come to your
rescue, on account of your devotion
to me." She, at once, out of gratitude, joined the Order of St. Francis.

27.—In Company with St. Anthony.

A child had fallen into the water,
and its mother, who, from a distance,
saw the accident, cried out: "Oh!
St. Anthony, help." She looked in

vain for her son, but at last, discovering him among the reeds in the
river, succeeded in saving him.   He
was not at all hurt, but laughed
heartily.   On being asked the cause
of his merriment, he replied: "I was
playing with St. Anthony, who told
the water not to harm me, and I like
playing with him."

28.—Boys Playing in a Mill Stream.

A nobleman had promised to make
every year a pilgrimage to the tomb
of St. Anthony, in thanksgiving for
his having obtained for him the birth
of a lovely boy, the darling of his
heart.   When the child was old
enough, he used to accompany his
parents to Padua.   But one year, just
as they were about starting, the boy
fell ill, and the father went alone.   In
a few days he was quite well again, and

one day went out with his little companions to play in the dry bed of a
mill stream, near the fields. Whilst
they were amusing themselves, the
water was suddenly turned on, and no
trace of the ten children could be
found. The grief of the distracted
mothers on hearing the news of this
accident, can easily be imagined. In
the meantime the count returned from
Padua, and his first thought was to
ask for his son. At first no one dared
tell him the truth, but soon it eked out.
In the midst of his anguish, on learning this news, he had recourse to St.
Anthony and said to him: "My dear,
hoiy protector, it rests with you to restore to me the child you gave me, for
surely you will not take him back."
After this prayer, he rose from his
knees, certain that his heavenly friend
would not desert him. He was right,

for hearing the noise of boyish laughter, he looked out of his window and saw the merry little band of children, with his son in their midst, returning home from the meadow. It would be impossible here to describe the feelings of the happy parents. The boys, on being questioned how they had spent their time, replied they had had lots of fun, but knew nothing of what had happened. In this manner did the saint reward the pilgrimage of his pious votaries, by saving the lives of those little ones so dear to them.

29.—Back from Paradise.

A Spanish princess had died, and her funeral was already ordered, but the queen mother, who had a great devotion to St. Anthony, now that all human assistance was of no avail had recourse to his intercession. In her grief she never left the corpse of her beloved daughter, and, with streaming eyes, said to our divine Lord: "It will not cost you more to raise my daughter from the dead than it did when you raised Lazarus from the grave, after being buried four days." St. Anthony in heaven joined in her supplications, and to the joy and astonishment of all present, the young girl arose, and said to her mother: "Dearest mother, while you were praying to St. Anthony, I was in heaven, amid the choir of virgins, and I so clearly understood all the vanities of this world that I entreated God not to hear your prayers. He replied He could not refuse any favor to His servant, St. Anthony, and that also, on account of your earnest prayers, I must return to this world, to change your grief

into joy, promising me, at the same
time, I should return to my place
among the blessed in a fortnight."
Everything happened as she predicted.
A fortnight afterwards she expired,
and went back to enjoy forever the
presence of God.

30.—Assassins Frightened.

A priest in Padua, who had a great
devotion to St. Anthony, had several
enemies, who were eagerly watching
for an opportunity to destroy him.
One night, whilst they were waiting in
ambush for the priest, a Franciscan
monk suddenly placed himself a few
steps before them. Finding he had no
intention to move, one of them surlily
ordered him in loud voice to move on.
The Father gently, but firmly, replied,
"Go your way yourselves; I shall re-

main here." Seeing him so determined, another rudely asked him:
"Pray, who are you?" "I am," he
replied, "the saint of Padua." Upon
which, as if struck down by some in-
visible power, they fell on their faces
to the ground, just at the time when
the priest, who, suspecting nothing,
passed by, and was informed by his
holy patron of the danger he had escaped. The would-be assassins, filled
with remorse, humbly begged his forgiveness, and related how the great
St. Anthony, without being called
upon, watches over those who trust in
him.

31.—A Strong Shield.

The following incident took place
at Puglia, in the kingdom of Naples,
before so many witnesses that the

news of it soon spread all over the country. A peasant boy was digging a hole beside a steep rock, when it fell suddenly, carrying the boy with it in its fall. His younger brother, who had seen the accident, ran to tell his mother of it. Her first thought was to call on St. Anthony to help her, as well as those who were going to the rescue of her child. At last, in the presence of an immense crowd, the stones were removed, and to the great astonishment of all present, not only was the boy alive, but he had not even a scratch on his face or head. Being asked how he had been able to save himself, he replied: "As soon as you, mother, began praying to St. Anthony, he at once came and shielded me with his hand, so that not only did the sharp stones not fall on me, but I could breathe freely."

32.—Dragged by a Mule.

Once Father Colnago, S. J., who had a great devotion to St. Anthony of Padua, was returning to Palermo from Mazzara, in Sicily, accompanied by one of the Brothers, and saying his breviary. He had just come to that verse in the canticle of the young men in the fiery furnace: "Praise the Lord, all His works," when his mule, which was considered a quiet animal, took fright, and broke the bridle. The Father was thrown out of the saddle, and dragged for a considerable dis- tance over a rough and ragged road, with his feet caught in the stirrups. He went on all the time saying his pray- ers, as if nothing was wrong. At last the mule was stopped. On getting up from the ground he told his compan-

ion, who expected to find him either
dead or seriously injured: "It is to the
prayers of St. Anthony that I owe my
safety."

33.—A Scoffer Changed into an Admirer.

The following account of a most
extraordinary conversion, through the
intercession of St. Anthony, was written by a gentleman living in Venice,
A. D. 1677.

For many years he had been a Cal-
vinist, and on his way back from
Rome. visited Padua, where he heard
so much about the miracles of St. Anthony, that, having no faith in them,
he was sick of hearing them mentioned. Curiosity, however, made him
visit the "Church del Santo," considered one of the most beautiful in the
city. Whilst looking at the chapel

under which the body of the saint lay,
he could not help thinking of the necessity of saving his soul, and on
drawing near the sarcophagus, he began reading an account of the miracles
engraved on it. He was so struck by
the story of the mule adoring the
Blessed Sacrament that he could
not forget it. Trusting that travel
would drive these thoughts, which
pursued him night and day, away,
he left Padua and started for
Milan, but to no purpose. At last,
yielding to grace, he became a fervent
Catholic, and a devout client of St.
Anthony. He was often heard to say
he would rather lose all the goods of
this world and suffer any amount of
torture than desert the Catholic
Church.

34.—A Glass as hard as a Rock.

A Protestant soldier named Alear-
dino Sansalvatore went to see his
family at Padua. One day, whilst at
table, the conversation naturally ran
on the miracles of St. Anthony of
Padua, recently deceased. Full of
pride, and not believing a word of
them, the heretic scoffingly said: "I
will become a Catholic, if this glass,
which I hold in my hand, does not
break into pieces when I throw it
against that stone," pointing to a large
stone not far off. No sooner said
than done. He threw the glass with
such violence that the stone against
which it was thrown was shivered to
pieces, whilst the glass remained unin-
jured. Astounded at the sight of this
miracle, he became a Catholic and

made a present of the glass to the
Franciscan monastery at Padua,
where it may still be seen.

35.—A Wish Granted.

A lay Sister of the Order of the
Poor Ladies of Mount Olivet
approached the corpse of St. Anthony
whilst it was still lying unburied
in the church, and reverently kiss-
ing his hand, implored him, in
her simplicity, to have her purgatory here on earth, so that she
might go straight to heaven at her
death. Her petition was granted. On
her return home she was seized with
such violent pains all over her body
that her screams could be heard all
over the convent. At night they grad-
ually abated, and she was able the next
day to get up and go to the refectory.

She had hardly sat down, before they returned with such intensity that the mother abbess was compelled to send her to the infirmary. Here she had again recourse to the saint, begging of him this time to cure her. Remembering a poor woman had a piece of his habit, she sent for it, placed it on her body and instantly recovered.

36.—A Poor Clare Cured.

Sister Victoria, a poor Clare, belonging to the monastery at Vienna, certainly deserved her name, owing to her great confidence in God, even when laboring under the greatest difficulties. On one occasion, after being bled, one of the sinews of her right arm was so injured that the whole arm swelled up and became so in-

flamed that her life was despaired of.
The pain, which was intense, never
ceased, and the doctor lost every hope
of saving her. Victoria alone, full
of confidence in God and in the intercession of her patron, St. Anthony,
felt convinced of the contrary. Instead of joining in the prayers of those
surrounding her bedside, she repeated
the *Te Deum* and antiphons. On the
eve of the feast of St. Thomas, the
inflammation had so increased that the
Sisters expected every moment the bell
to be tolled for her decease. Towards
midnight a slight improvement was
noticed in the state of the patient,
which continued, so that in a few days
she was able to move her hand without
danger. On her recovery, she informed the prioress of what had taken
place. About midnight the mother
abbess had brought two Franciscan

monks to her bedside, St. Anthony,
and St. Bernardin of Sienna. One
repeated the antiphons to her, and ordered her to stretch out her hand; the
other had blessed her in the name of
our dear Lord, and she was instantly
cured.

37.—Places Exchanged.

During the Middle Ages, leprosy
was very prevalent in Italy, and St.
Bonaventure used often, in the antiphons, to implore the assistance of St.
Anthony to obtain the cure of those
attacked by this dire disease.

The following incident proves how
powerful his intercession was: A poor
leper, having heard of the miracles
worked by St. Anthony, determined,
full of confidence in his intercession,
to go and pray on his tomb. On his

way to the church, he met a soldier,
who scoffingly said to him: "Where
are you going, you simpleton? Do
you think the ashes and bones of that
Brother can heal you? Go, tell him
with my compliments, I am not afraid
of death, and he can send me your
leprosy if he likes." The leper went
his way, not heeding the words of the
scoffer, but full of trust in the saint,
and kneeling before his shrine soon
fell into a beautiful sleep, during which
he dreamt he saw St. Anthony, who
kindly said to him: "Arise, brother,
you are cured; go, give your crutches
to the soldier; he sadly needs them."
On awaking, he found it was no
illusion; he was perfectly cured, and
went at once, as he had been bidden,
to seek the soldier, whom he found
covered with leprosy. Giving him
his crutches, said: "I am cured; my

saint has told me to give you my crutches."

In this manner, two miracles were wrought: one of mercy, the other of chastisement. As for the soldier, the sight of this miracle touched his heart, and, full of repentance, he allowed himself to be carried to the shrine of the saint, hoping he would have compassion on him. Nor was he mistaken, for after his promising to lead a better life and become a good Catholic, he was also restored to health. He never forgot his promise, and became a most devout client of St. Anthony.

38.—"Dost Thou Know Me?"

Aldonisia, the daughter of Queen Taraxia, of Portugal, lay on a sick-bed, given up by all, save the queen mother, who could not believe her child was going to die, for she felt confident that St. Anthony, whose devout client she was, would cure her darling. "Come," said she to him in her anguish, "come, you were born in this land, come and obtain, through your powerful intercession, the cure of my child." Shortly after midnight, the young girl fell asleep, and the saint, appearing to her, said: "Dost thou know me? I am St. Anthony, and am come here at the request of your mother. You can have your choice, either to be with me to-day in heaven without passing through the flames of purgatory, or to recover and return to your mother." The child chose the health of the body and was immediately cured. Taking hold of the cord of St. Anthony, she cried out to her mother: "See, mother, here is St.

Anthony, who has come to cure me."
The queen and her suite rushed to the
bedside of the princess, and on finding
her child cured, the mother fell on her
knees to thank God and St. Anthony.

39.—A Son Restored to his Parents.

The following miracle took place at
Rome, in the month of March, 1683:
Don Nicholas Grassi, the president of
the royal board of administration at
Naples, having to go to Rome, took
with him his wife and only son. They
had scarcely reached the city before
the child fell dangerously ill, and was
given up by the doctors. His mother,
a devout client of St. Anthony, full of
confidence in his intercession, implored the saint to befriend her on this
trying occasion. Suddenly at about
three o'clock in the afternoon of
Shrove Tuesday, she heard her

son calling out to the saint. She
immediately ran to the sick-bed,
but he, waving her away with his
hand, distinctly cried out: "Anthony."
She again asked him whom he was
calling, and this time he replied: "I
saw a monk in a dark habit; it must
have been St. Anthony himself, for he
held in one hand some lovely red and
white roses, and in the other a book,
on which a beautiful boy was standing." From that time the child got better, and in a few days was completely
cured. On being taken to a church,
where there was a picture of the
saint, he at once pointed it out to his
mother, saying: "Look, mother, there
is the monk who appeared to me during my illness and cured me." Every
time he met a Franciscan Father, he
would exclaim: "There is a monk who
wears the same habit as St. Anthony."

40.—Gangrene Cured.

In 1674, Count Mirola, the com-
mander-in-chief of the papal army, sent
to reinforce the Venetians in the war
against the Turks, was seriously
wounded in the ankle at the siege of
Sebenico. In the hope of saving his
life, the foot was amputated, but in
spite of this, gangrene set in. The
count, full of confidence in the intercession of St. Anthony, sent for
one of his pictures, and placing it on
the wounded limb, said: "Although
I am only a miserable sinner, knowing
how good thou art to us, I am certain,
dear St. Anthony, of being cured
through thy powerful intercession."
The count's confidence was not misplaced; in a short time the wound was
completely healed, and soon the news

of this fresh miracle spread far and wide.

41.—"Take Courage."

Such were the words which St. Anthony himself addressed, in 1682, to a poor man dying at Naples, of dropsy in the head. Emmanuel Caravascione, in spite of being given over by the doctors, and speechless, never lost hope, and although those round his bedside were expecting him every moment to breathe his last, he was himself silently imploring the saint to intercede for him and to come to his rescue. It was not in vain. About midnight, St. Anthony appeared to him and said: "Take courage, friend. I will help you," and disappeared. The sick man at once recovered his speech, called his wife, and, relating all that had just taken place, told her to go

to the Franciscan church and
earnestly implore the saint's intercession. To this the poor woman
gladly acceded, immediately going
barefooted to the church, where
she had several Masses, together with
the antiphons of the saint, said in his
honor. On her return home, she
found the doctor perfectly astonished
at the marked improvement in the
state of the patient. Whilst he was
thus talking with her, her little three-
year-old boy, who had been staying in
the sick-room, suddenly ran up to her,
pulling at her dress, wanting her to
come and see St. Anthony, who was
talking with his father. Not paying
attention to what the little one said,
she continued her conversation with
the doctor and then went back to the
sick-room, where, to her great astonishment, she found her husband per-

fectly recovered from his illness. "Oh, mamma," said the child, reproachfully, "why did you not come sooner? See, St. Anthony is gone."

42.—A Good Name Restored.

In 1641, a parish priest in the Tyrol was falsely accused by some of his parishioners of having committed a dreadful crime, and denounced to his bishop. The priest, conscious of his innocence, did not hesitate for a moment, anticipating the summons, but, after appearing before the consistory, he was condemned and sent to prison.

Finding his good name gone, and that there seemed no chance of his obtaining redress from man, he did not lose heart, but at once wrote to St. Anthony, imploring his assistance. As it was impossible for him to take the letter to the monastery at Kattern, he sent it by a messenger, begging the monks to place it on the altar dedicated to the saint, which they did.

St. Anthony, ever the friend of the persecuted, came at once to the rescue of his devout suppliant, and soon made the judges discover the injustice of the accusation. The sentence of imprisonment pronounced against him was at once annulled, and he was honorably reinstated in his former parish. His calumniators, in order to save themselves from heavier penalties, were forced not only to retract their accusations, and pay all the expenses of the trial, but also to perform great works of charity.

43.—A Lunatic Cured.

In 1701, Herr Franz Zallinger, a gentleman highly respected in Botzen, was suddenly seized with madness while attending the services at the Franciscan church, and became so convulsed that it required several strong men to carry him out of the terror-stricken congregation, and to put him in one of the cells of the monastery, where he had to be closely watched. His brother George, a devout client of St. Anthony, had at once recourse to the saint's intercession in behalf of the unfortunate lunatic, who was immediately cured and restored to his family.

A magnificent *ex voto*, in the form of a large silver heart, was placed by the grateful family on the altar of St.

Anthony, at Kattern, as a memento of
this miraculous cure.

44.—A happy Death Obtained.

A Spanish nobleman, noted for the
cordial and respectful welcome he gave
to the Franciscans who asked hos-
pitality from him, lay at the point of
death, when two Franciscan Fathers
came and wanted to see him. On
hearing of their arrival, he immediately
ordered them to be shown up to his
room, and said to them: "I have always longed for two of your religious
to come and assist me in my last moments, and God has heard my prayer;
do, pray, I entreat you, remain with me
till all is over."

"Most willingly," replied the elder
of the two monks, whose hands
were marked with the stigmata; "we

are here for that purpose. I am Francis and my companion is Anthony. We have only come down from heaven in order to bring you back with us." What a consolation for a man on his death-bed!

45.—Crushed by the Fall of a Tree.

In the year 1666, one of the laborers of a nobleman, called Johannes Kaspar Inderman, residing at Kurtasch, in the Tyrol, experienced the protection of St. Anthony in a most wonderful manner. One day whilst engaged in felling down a large tree, just after giving the last stroke his foot slipped, and the whole weight of the immense trunk fell on his body, rendering him unconscious. The wife of the nobleman at once, on hearing of the accident, had recourse to the intercession

of St. Anthony, promising to have two
Masses said in his chapel at Kattern,
if he would only save the life of the
poor fellow. The promise was hardly
made before the man got up unhurt.
Out of gratitude to St. Anthony, he
placed an *ex voto* in his chapel at Kat·
tern.

46.—Marriage Portion.

In 1649, St. Anthony did a great
act of kindness to a poor girl. The
mother, pressed by extreme poverty,
wanted to sell her beautiful daughter
for money. The unhappy girl, in her
anguish, went and knelt before the
picture of St. Anthony, in the Franciscan church, imploring him, weeping bitterly, to save her honor. In the
midst of her prayer, the saint stretched
out his hand and handing a note to
her, said: "Go to the bishop's admin-

istrator, and tell him in my name to give you for your marriage portion as much money as this paper weighs." Full of joy, she at once obeyed, and presented the note to the aforesaid gentleman. He at first laughed at her but after putting the paper in one side of the scales, and finding it weighed two hundred silver crowns, remembered a promise he had made the year before to give the above-named sum of money, as a marriage portion, to a poor girl. He at once handed the sum over to her, thus saving her from dishonor.

47.—Saved from Suicide.

Discord is the greatest of all evils which can enter into a house. Union in wedlock, and in one's family makes life a real paradise on earth. Heaven

cannot exist without harmony. Hell
is one continual discord.

A most unhappy family lived in one
of the small villages of Portugal. The
husband, not content, on coming
home at night, with calling his wife
bad names, used to beat her, kick her,
and even threaten to turn her out of
doors. The cause of such conduct
can be easily guessed; he used to stay
out late at night and frequented bad
company. The poor woman, at last
despairing of her husband turning
over a new leaf, determined to destroy
herself. One night, after her husband had gone to his usual haunts,
just as she was about fetching the
rope which was to put an end to her
misery in this world, she heard a
knock at the door. On opening it,
two Franciscan Fathers humbly asked
if she could give them a night's lodg-

ing, saying: "We are come a great distance, and are called Francis and Anthony." On hearing these words, the poor woman exclaimed: "Oh, what beautiful names! They are the names of two saints I love very dearly. Do, pray, come in, reverend Fathers; you are indeed welcome." She at once set about getting everything ready, so as to make them as comfortable as possible. While listening to their conversation about heavenly things, at supper, all thoughts of despair and suicide vanished, a feeling of peace and gratitude stole over her heart, making her thank God for having sent her such guests. As soon as the strangers seemed to be preparing to retire to rest, she withdrew to a little room, and there, falling on her knees, humbly implored God's forgiveness, promising

Him, for the future, never to yield to despair, being certain that He who is constantly watching over those who place their whole trust in Him, never permits anything to happen to them but for their greater good.

Whilst still on her knees, she heard her husband enter the house. But oh, how changed! Instead of beginning to curse and swear at her, as soon as he saw her, he fell at her feet, his face bathed in tears, and humbly entreated forgiveness. What could have changed him so? It was soon explained. Immediately after the poor woman had left the Fathers, they had appeared to the cruel husband, and, after sternly reproaching him with his crimes, threatened him with eternal damnation if he did not at once amend. "Richly, indeed, do you deserve to be among the damned, after committing crime upon crime. You will certainly be cast into hell in three days if you do not at once quit this place. Repent of your sins, confess, do penance for them and amend. Hasten home to your wife, ask her for the cord with which she was about to destroy herself, and beg her to forgive you. Tell her the two monks she received and welcomed into her house to-night are no other than St. Francis and St. Anthony." It would be impossible to describe the joy and gratitude of this now reconciled couple towards the two great saints who had been the instruments used by God to save them, soul and body. They at once, both of them, approached the Sacraments of Penance and of the Altar, and from henceforth led lives which were a foretaste of heaven.

48.—Great Harvest.

A poor woman living near Padua had only a single field of wheat, which was so devoured by sparrows that hardly an ear of corn could be seen. No sooner had she driven them off one part of the field than they flew to another, with the greatest impudence. Finding her labor useless, she had recourse to St. Anthony, and, asking him to take care of her field, promised to visit his tomb nine times. Certain of his protection, she at once began her novena, and during that time left the field entirely under his care. After the novena was finished, she went to see how things were going on, and to her surprise found that not a sparrow was to be seen. That year she had a finer harvest than she ever had before.

49.—The Storm Ceases and the Sea becomes Calm.

A Maronite bishop, Timothy di Sarca, had left Mesopotamia to go to Rome. The coast of Ostia was already seen in the distance, when suddenly a terrific hurricane arose on the Tyrrhenian sea, the ship being tossed about like a ball and her mast broken. All hopes of reaching land were given up, even by the oldest sailors, who only thought of preparing themselves for death. The good bishop, a devout client of St. Anthony, alone did not lose courage, and urged the passengers and crew to have recourse to St. Anthony, and to promise, did they reach the land, to burn a candle in his honor. To this all unanimously agreed. Immediately the storm ceased, the waters became as smooth as glass, and the vessel glided into port, driven by a favorable wind.

During his stay at Rome, the same bishop experienced another favor from his heavenly friend and benefactor. The Propaganda had given him a bill of exchange, in order to help him on his journey. Somehow or other, just as he was going to leave the city, it got mislaid and could not be found. In this dilemma he had at once recourse to his holy patron, and, having said Mass in his honor, begging of him to assist him, he returned to the house at which he was staying, where, to his great surprise, he found the bill lying on his table in his room.

50.—"She is all Right Now."

A ship, heavily laden with silk from Catalonia, had just reached the coast of Sicily, when a terrific storm arose, and the vessel was driven back to sea with such violence that she became perfectly unmanageable. Everybody on board thought they were lost, except one of the crew, who, in a loud voice, called upon St. Anthony to come to their rescue, saying: "Dear St. Anthony, become the pilot of this vessel; we hand her over to you." Immediately, on the sailors responding to this appeal, St. Anthony was seen at the helm, and, smiling at the crew, addressed them thus: "Let the vessel go by herself, she is all right now," after which he disappeared, and a gentle breeze drove the ship into harbor, without mast or rudder.

51.—The Beacon.

The remembrance of the protection
of this great thaumaturgus is still preserved in the lagoons. Shortly after
the canonization of the saint, a gon-
dola containing more than twenty-six
persons, whilst passing through Venice, during a night which was pitch
dark, was caught in a sudden squall,
and the boat was struck by the wind
with such violence that for a moment
the people in it did not know
whether it was capsized or not.   In
this dilemma, they all cried out with
one voice: "St. Anthony, help us; St.
Anthony, help us."   At once, in the
midst of the darkness, a bright light
was seen, and they found the boat was
close to the little island of San Marco
Piccolo, where they were safely
landed.   The light then disappeared,

and the rescued party fell on their knees to thank their heavenly benefactor.

52.—The Singer in the Boat.

During a violent storm, a poor fisherman in Portugal, whose sole means of getting an honest livelihood depended on his boat, had the misfortune to see it break from its moorings and drift into the open sea. In his distress, he at once appealed to St. Anthony. Two days afterwards, one of his neighbors came and told him how some young men, during a terrific storm, had seen a boat in the open sea, with no other occupant than a Franciscan monk at the helm, who was singing beautiful hymns. Struck by the coincidence, the poor man at once ran to the shore, where, to his great joy, he found his boat stranded on the beach.

53.—Chains as an Altar Decoration.

In the year 1672, a poor man, living in Cracovia, Poland, was unjustly accused of murder and condemned to the rack. This punishment, most terrible in itself, was frequently resorted to in the Middle Ages to force suspected criminals to confess the crimes of which they were accused, and it is certain the most innocent have declared themselves guilty of offences of which they had not even the remotest idea, rather than undergo this terrible torture a second time. Once a Capuchin Father was known, through fear of being again placed on this cruel instrument, to confess having struck Our Lord whilst He was hanging on the cross. What happened to the priest also happened to the poor Pole, who, whilst stretched on the rack, finding death preferable to what he was suffering, although quite innocent, declared he was guilty. On being taken back to prison, he began preparing himself for death, by receiving the sacraments of the Church, giving abundant alms and recommending himself especially to St. Anthony. The good saint would not permit his devout client to suffer such a disgraceful death, and on the night before his execution appeared to him, opened the prison gates, and, breaking his chains, ordered him to take them to his judges, so as to have his sentence revoked. The proofs of his innocence were too palpable to be doubted; the man was set free, and at once, out of gratitude, placed

the chains on the altar of the
saint, where they are still to be seen.

54.—St. Antbony is Never Invoked in Vain.

The celebrated Jesuit Father, Daniel Papebroch, relates the following
incident which took place at Antwerp,
in his youth, and which he never forgot: It happened that a woman in
business who had received a note of
hand from the head of a mercantile
house could not find it anywhere, just
at the time it became due. The loss
of it did not at first trouble her very
much, as having had dealing with
the above-named house for several
years, and her honesty being known
to the firm, she felt certain payment
would not be refused. She was mistaken; not only was she informed that
the money had been already paid, but

she was grossly insulted, which hurt even more than the loss of the money. She therefore determined to consult a well-known soothsayer as to the best means of finding the lost note. Fortunately for her, she met on her way the mother of Father Papebroch, to whom she related what had taken place. After hearing her story, the lady strongly advised her to have a Mass said to St. Anthony, to which she at once agreed, and assisted at it herself. On her return home, she found a servant waiting for her, who informed her that his master, believing what she said to be true, was quite prepared to pay her the money without the note being produced.

55.—King Charles II. of England.

In 1655, Charles II., who had been banished from England, went to re-

side at Cologne. Whilst there, the
little gold and silver plate he had, and
which he greatly valued, was stolen.
In spite of being a Protestant, he sent
one of the gentlemen of his suite to
beg of the Friars Minor to pray for
his intentions. The following day,
Father Werner Burich, a highly respected priest, whilst passing through
the church, noticed a stranger beckon-
ing to him and pointing to a confes-
sional. Thinking something was
wrong, he went at once to the place,
and found there the sack containing
the lost plate. He immediately sent
for the superior of the monastery,
Father Thomas Martine, who ordered
two of the Brothers to restore the plate
to the rightful owner. The king, delighted at having recovered his lost
property, ordered an account of it to

be published, which he attested and signed with his own hand.

56.—The Grateful Captain.

In 1674, a Swiss captain, stationed at Dunkirk, in French Flanders, one night on retiring to rest, put his purse, containing sixty gold doubloons, under his pillow, but on awakening the next morning could not find them; the purse had disappeared. He at once went to ask the assistance of St. Anthony, and had a Mass said in his honor at the Franciscan church. During the Offertory, somebody knocked at the door of the monastery. On the porter opening it, a soldier, accompanied by another man, gave him the purse, which the Brother at first hesitated to receive. The soldier insisted, and, throwing it at his feet, exclaimed: "I did not steal the purse," and disappeared. When Mass was over, the money was restored to the captain, who, out of gratitude, made a present of the greater part of it to the monastery. A picture, commemorating this and other miracles worked by the saint, was placed in his chapel.

57.—A Child Stolen.

In 1720, a poor woman left her little four-year-old child alone in her garden, surrounded by high walls, as she was obliged to go to Botzen on business. On her return from town, she went to fetch her little girl, who was nowhere to be found. Full of anguish, she immediately made a pilgrimage to St. Anthony's chapel, at Kattern, and on coming home, found the little one safe and sound in the house. On being questioned by her mother, she replied: "Whilst you were

away, a man climbed over the wall
of our garden, and carried me to the
top of a big hill, but I had not been
long there before a priest found me,
and brought me home, telling me I
must be a very good little girl and always say my prayers and mind what
you tell me, which I certainly shall
try." The grateful mother easily
guessed that the good priest could
be no other than St. Anthony.

58.—Erysipelas Cured through Invok= ing St. Anthony.

The youngest son of John Amaldus
von Buren, a lad of thirteen, owing to
a severe attack of erysipelas, had to
have the knee bone of his right leg
taken out. In spite of this painful operation, cancer set in, and the only
hopes of saving the sufferer's life was
by amputating the diseased limb. The
boy, on hearing this, asked for a pic-

ture of St. Anthony, and full of confidence in his powerful intercession,
implored him to take pity on him and
cure him; promising if he did so, to
make a pilgrimage to his shrine at
Padua, and always to wear a gray
dress in his honor. No sooner was
the promise made than he felt himself
perfectly cured. Shortly afterwards
he started for Padua to fulfil his vow,
and was able to kneel at the altar of
the saint without feeling any pain.
Those who had seen him during his
illness could hardly believe in the
cure, but, after carefully examining
the knee, they found to their great
astonishment no trace of the bone having been taken out.

59.—Tbe Bisbop's Ring.

Don Ignatius Martiques, Bishop of
Cordova, had a great devotion to St.

Anthony and received many favors from him. Once he lost his bishop's ring, which he had received at his consecration, and naturally, for this reason, the loss of it greatly troubled him. He at once had several Masses said for his intention, but the saint seemed to have turned a deaf ear. One day whilst at table with several gentlemen, the conversation ran upon the miracles the saint was working, and which filled the whole world with astonishment. The bishop also spoke about the many favors he had received, and how greatly he trusted the dear saint, but added: "I am just now rather inclined to quarrel with him, for in spite of my repeatedly asking him, he has not yet given me back my ring." Hardly had he uttered these words before the ring, to the astonishment of all present, fell on the table, as if coming from the ceiling, and every one joined in giving three cheers for St. Anthony.

60.—The Manuscript Ready for the Press.

The Dominican bishop, Ambrosius Catherinus, as renowned for his virtue as for his great learning, has written several books, among others one bearing the title of "Honor due to the Saints," from which the following anecdote is extracted: The bishop, on his way home from Toulouse, after travelling a considerable distance, discovered that a valuable manuscript, ready for printing, was missing. He immediately retraced his steps, in the hopes of finding it, and even took the trouble of asking the governor of the city to assist him. Finding earthly aid of no avail, he had recourse to St. Anthony, promising to mention this favor in his book, were the manuscript found. Full of these thoughts, he resumed his journey and on the road met a stranger, who, drawing near to him, asked if he had not lost a manuscript. The bishop replied in the affirmative, and gave a description of the lost treasure. Upon which the man, after returning it to him, showed him the place where he had dropped it. Full of gratitude, the bishop faithfully kept his word, and gave an account of his loss in the book, which was printed at Lyons, 1541.

61.—Beard during Mass.

John Comez Cano, chamberlain to the Duke of Brabant, had a great lawsuit to carry on in the Senate House, but unfortunately some very import-

ant documents had been mislaid, without which the case would be lost. In
this predicament, John Comez Cano's
only hope was to make an appeal to
St. Anthony and implore his assistance, promising, in return, to have
three Masses said in his honor. Full
of these thoughts, he went to the
Franciscan church in Brussels, and,
while on his way to the chapel, met one
of the Fathers in the cloisters, who,
looking at him most benevolently,
asked in Spanish the cause of his sad-
ness. On being informed of it, he
said: "Go and hear a Mass in honor
of St. Anthony, and you will receive
the lost documents to-morrow," which
was, in fact, the case. The lawsuit
was gained and an *ex voto* was placed
in the chapel of the saint to commem-
orate the miracle, which happened in
1646.

62.—An Ant employed as Porter.

St. Anthony is ever ready to help those who fully trust in him, even in the most trifling matters. Supposing you lose a key, only ask St Anthony and he will certainly find it for you. The following incident clearly proves the truth of this assertion: A lay Capuchin Brother had a rosary which, for the many indulgences attached to it, he greatly prized. One day he accidentally broke the string on which the beads were strung, so that they were scattered all over the ground. He at once began to pick them up, but to his great vexation, one was missing, and not being able to find it he at once said a prayer to St. Anthony, which was no sooner finished than to his great astonishment he saw an ant coming with great difficulty towards him, carrying on her back the lost bead. Filled with gratitude, the good Brother wept for joy at the sight of the kindness of his dear saint.

63.—Returned at Midnight.

In 1664 a rich merchant from Augsburg sent his confidential servant on business to St. Andrew's market, at Botzen, and gave him at the same time two hundred and thirty guldens in coin and several thousands in paper money, which were carefully packed up in his travelling bag. The servant being obliged to go to Trent on business, returned by way of Tramin. Worn out by his long journey, and finding it impossible to proceed any further until he had rested a little, he lay down near the roadside close to Tramin, and

was soon fast asleep. On awaking, he
found his bag had disappeared. He
at once made use of every means he
possibly could to discover the thief,
but finding it useless, went to Kattern
on the 23d of November, and on seeing the superior of the Franciscans,
informed him of his loss, at the same
time asking for three Masses and
other prayers to be said in honor of
St. Anthony, and returned again to
Botzen, fully convinced that the
money would be found. In the meantime, the antiphons in honor of St.
Anthony were daily said by the choir
Brothers, in order to obtain his assistance. On the 13th of December,
whilst matins was being sung, a terrible noise was heard at the church door,
which increased so much that the
Brothers, greatly alarmed, went to see
what was the matter. Suddenly all

was silent, and, on their reaching the
door, they found it forced open and
inside a quantity of paper scattered
over the floor, together with two bags
of money, a pair of stockings and an
old veil, all of which was the stolen
property of the merchant, M. Morrell,
who was then staying at Botzen. On
his receiving the stolen things, he
found only twenty-one gulden and
thirty-eight kreuzers missing; out of
gratitude he had an *ex voto* placed in
the chapel, on which was a representation of the church door being forced
open, and bags of money being thrown
inside the church.

64.—The Victorious Admiral.

The very reverend Father Provincial Kuck, of the Franciscan province
of Bavaria, heard, himself, the follow-

ing incident related by Admiral Don
Mondemar, during his visit to Spain,
when convoked to the General Chapter, held at Murcia. The then reign-
ing King of Spain, Philip IV., determined to send a fleet to recapture
Oran from the Moors. Several at-
tempts had already been made, all of
which had failed, and the fortress was
considered impregnable. In spite of
everything the admiral could say, the
king persisted in his determination,
and, consequently, nothing remained
but to obey. On reaching Alicant,
Don Mondemar allowed his troops to
disembark, and availed himself of this
opportunity to visit the church of the
Franciscans, dedicated to St. Anthony,
where he placed the whole business in
his hands. With this intention, after
spending some time in prayer, he
called upon the superior, begging of

him to have the office of St. Anthony
said. This being ended, he, in the
presence of a great many people,
asked the Father Superior's permission to have a ladder placed before the
high altar, over which a life-size statue
of the saint stood. This granted, he
mounted the ladder and clothed the
statue with all the insignia of a Spanish
admiral in active service, and thus addressed the saint: "You, St. Anthony,
must capture Oran, for I am unable to
do so;" and laying his hand on the
head of the statue, continued: "You
are now the admiral, and I am only
your humble servant and soldier,
ready to obey your orders, for after
God, I place my whole trust in you."
This ceremony concluded, he came
down from the ladder and returned
with his men to the fleet, where they
embarked. As the squadron drew

near Oran, all waited anxiously for the enemy to begin the attack. Seeing no notice was taken of them, the admiral ordered his men to fire. Again no response from the citadel. At a loss to understand what this meant, the command was given to land the troops, and, to the great astonishment of every one, the city gates were wide open. Thinking this was a stratagem of the enemy, they proceeded very cautiously through the empty streets, which, like the fortress, were completely deserted. Here an old Moor was discovered, concealed in his house, and was immediately brought before the admiral, who demanded an explanation of this extraordinary behavior on the part of the garrison and inhabitants. "As soon," replied the old man, "as the Christian squadron appeared in sight, a legion of soldiers was seen in the air, led by a Franciscan monk, wearing all the insignia of an admiral on duty, who threatened to destroy every one of us if we did not at once leave the city." Terrified beyond description at this unexpected apparition, both citizens and garrison had fled in the greatest disorder.

It was in this way that, thanks to the assistance of St. Anthony, Mondemar captured the city of Oran, without shedding a drop of blood. He at once sent a dispatch to the king, informing him of all that had taken place. The statue, clothed with an admiral's insignia, is still to be seen at Alicant, but the miracle was only confirmed in Rome in 1770.

65.—Saved from the Scaffold.

A Franciscan Father, who lived at Naples in the monastery dedicated to

St. Lawrence, relates the following incident which took place in that city.
One stormy night a young fisherman
was sitting alone with his mother, in
his little cottage close to the sea, when
he heard, in the midst of the howling
of the wind, some one in great distress
calling for help. He immediately
went out and found a man mortally
wounded, lying close to his door. The
murderer had fled, but the coast-guard
had also heard the cries for help, and
seeing the young fisherman bending
over the dead man, naturally concluded he was guilty, and, in spite of
all his protestations, he was brought
before the judge and accused of murder.

His guilt was, in fact, only too evi-
dent; he had been found bending over
the corpse of a man, still warm. No
one else could be found in the neigh-

borhood, and there was only his mother who could prove his innocence, and what is a mother's evidence in such a case, even had she come in time? But the poor creature was so stunned by grief on hearing the accusation against her only son, that she reached the court just before the sentence of death was pronounced on her child. On hearing which, the wretched mother, in spite of all the rebuffs she received from the judge, persisted in asking him to spare her child's life. At last, weary of her importunities, and perhaps also in the hopes of getting rid of her, he informed her that if she could see the king, there was a small chance of a reprieve being obtained. Full of hope, the unhappy parent at once started upon her mission, but what appeared so easy was truly beset with difficulties. On reaching the palace she was told she must have a petition presented to the king, and who was to write that petition? When she at last succeeded in getting it done, it was far too late for her to obtain an audience of the king. Broken-hearted, she left the palace, and, as she was passing by the Church of St. Lawrence, she entered, and kneeling before the railings which separated St. Anthony's chapel from the rest of the church, she implored the saint's intercession in behalf of her unfortunate son. She would have remained there longer, had not the sacristan told her he must shut up the church, and then, in her despair, she threw her petition on his altar, crying out: "St. Anthony, St. Anthony, you must save my child." She then returned home, consoled and comforted, convinced that the saint would assist her.

It was ten o'clock in the evening, and the king, having some important work to do, had dismissed his attendants, when suddenly he heard a knock at his door and a young Franciscan monk entered. There was something so modest and prepossessing in his appearance that the king was perfectly fascinated, and received him most courteously. "Pardon me, sire," said the priest, "for disturbing you at so late an hour, but my errand is urgent and brooks of no delay, since the life of a fellow creature depends on it."

"Speak, Brother, how can I help you?"

"Your majesty has to-day signed a sentence of death on a young fisherman found near the corpse of a murdered man. Although appearances are against him, I declare to you he is innocent."

"When the law has pronounced judgment," answered the king, "it is not for me to change it or to presume that the sentence is unjust."

"I can swear to the innocence of my protégé," responded the monk. "All I entreat your majesty to do is to write the word 'reprieved' under this petition."

The Franciscan Father uttered these words in so determined a manner, that the king. in spite of himself, took up his pen, then paused, and said:

"Where do you come from?"

"From the Franciscan monastery, which bears the name of St. Lawrence."

"Even if I grant the reprieve, the young man will have been executed before it can reach the prison."

"I am well aware the time is short, but do what I ask you," replied

the Franciscan, firmly, pointing to
the petition. To this the king,
in spite of himself, acceded. The
petition was signed and, after
thanking his majesty, the monk disappeared. The king felt strangely
impressed by this visit, and, after remaining a few minutes absorbed in
thought, said to himself: "How could
this man have come here at this time
of night?" And sending for one of his
chamberlains, he asked who had in-
troduced the monk into the palace?
But neither the chamberlains nor any
one else had seen the monk enter, and
how he had done so remained a perfect
mystery. The king, finding it was
impossible to discover who the Father
was, determined to make inquiries at
the convent of St. Lawrence.

The following afternoon the king,
anxious to unravel the mystery of the

preceding night, went to the Franciscan monastery of St. Lawrence and, summoning all the community together, asked the superior whom he had sent the night before to the palace. To his astonishment the superior informed him he was not aware of any one being out of the monastery the preceding night. After carefully examining the faces of the monks and not finding the one he wanted, his majesty ordered the mother of the boy to be sent for, in order to question her as to the person to whom she had given the petition, and to while away the time inspected the monastery and then went to visit the church. After examining the different altars the king paused before the picture of St. Anthony and exclaimed, pointing it out to the superior:

"Ah! here is the priest who came to see me last night."

"Pardon me, sire, that Father is not under my jurisdiction," replied the superior.

It may be interesting for some to know how St. Anthony finished saving the young fisherman. The day after he was condemned to death was the one appointed for his execution, and early that same morning the public prosecutor, on awaking, found lying on the table near his bedside a paper containing the free pardon of the condemned, signed by the king and dated the night before. Thinking his servant had forgotten to give it to him the preceding evening, he hastily dressed himself and not daring to trust it to any one, for fear of it not reaching the prison authorities in time, took it himself to the jail. The surprise of the poor youth on seeing the royal official enter his cell, bringing with him not only the reprieve, but also the order for him to return to his mother, can be very easily imagined.

This occurrence soon spread all over Naples, and St. Anthony of Padua was chosen to be one of the patron saints of the city.

66.—A Choir Master without Employment.

For some time a choir master had vainly sought employment in Rome and Naples in order to procure the bare necessaries of life for his little family. On the 13th of June they were on the verge of starvation, and the poor man, in order to obtain the assistance of St. Anthony, approached

the holy Sacraments of Penance and
of the Altar, and heard several Masses
in his honor. On leaving the church a
stranger came up to him, and placed
sufficient money in his hands to satisfy his most pressing necessities.
But the good saint's favors did not
cease here. When he came home, his
wife, with a beaming countenance,
told him how an unknown benefactor
had sent his servant with enough food
to last them several weeks; and that
very day a letter came from Spoleto
offering him the post of music director
in the choir of the cathedral, which
was, of course, accepted. The grateful family never afterwards omitted re-
citing the antiphons in honor of the
saint. The last line,

Dicant Paduani,

is an everlasting testimony of the
wonderful manner in which St. An-

thony still watches over Padua. For six hundred years he has justly been considered its patron and protector. In every direction churches have been built, altars erected, and pious and charitable institutions founded in his honor. The citizens are almost daily eye witnesses of the marvellous power God has bestowed on His faithful servant. Thousands of pilgrims, from every part of the world, are constantly flocking to his shrine, either to thank him for past blessings or implore his aid. His altar is so covered with *ex votos* that it has been found necessary to set a room aside to receive the treasures which his grateful clients are constantly sending to his shrine.

67.—A Costly Ex Voto.

The Franciscan architect, Father
Valentine, a native of Worms, who
built the magnificent church dedicated
to St. Anthony, at Padua, related the
following incident, which took place
in the year 1871:

A Portuguese prince had long been
wishing for a son to inherit his vast
possessions. At last, after promising
a present of a silver statue of the holy
Child to the above-mentioned church,
a son was born. Filled with gratitude,
he ordered a statue of solid silver to
be cast of the same weight as the infant
prince. Fearing, on account of the
persecution of religious houses in
Italy, it might not fall into the right
hands, he forwarded it to Rome, by a
special escort, where it was delivered
over to Pope Pius IX. His Holi-

ness immediately sent for Father Valentine, ordering him to place it in the newly erected church of St. Anthony, at Padua, where it is still to be seen.

Few among the rich or learned of this age of incredulity and unbelief, in the pride of their hearts, place any faith in miracles. Let us not allow ourselves to be ranked among their number, but rather, like those believers in the Gospel, thank God He has given such power to men, and more especially to His faithful servant, St. Anthony.

60.—The Franciscan Church of St. Anthony in the Tyrol.

It has been the design of God to glorify His faithful servant, St. Anthony, by spreading his devotion, not only in Germany, France, Italy and

Spain, but throughout the whole
Catholic world. It is not here my intention to mention the names of the
principal places where this great saint
is honored, but simply to give an account of the origin of the pilgrimage
to the Church of St. Anthony at Kattern in the Tyrol.

In 1638, the ruined castle of Rot-
tenburg and grounds adjoining it
were conceded to the Franciscan
Fathers of the Tyrolese reformed
Province, for the purpose of building
a monastery, which, to the great joy
of the inhabitants of the neighboring
country, was completed in 1643. The
picture for the altar dedicated to St.
Anthony of Padua, was destined by
divine Providence, on account of the
many favors, spiritual and temporal,
which the devout clients of the saint
were to receive at this favored spot,

to be the means of making the monastery known far and wide.

A nobleman, Christopher Ulrich von Bach, was to be the instrument chosen by God to procure this miraculous picture. He had in 1638, thanks to the protection of the saint, escaped a most dangerous plot laid by his enemies. Filled with gratitude, he determined, at his own cost, to erect in the church of Kattern an altar dedicated to St. Anthony. It was found, after the altar had been set in its proper place, that a picture of the saint was wanting. God, desirous of spreading the devotion to His faithful servant, sent an unknown painter to Herr von Bach, who had just gone on a pilgrimage to Padua, to ask permission to paint a picture for him. The nobleman, being a stranger in the city, and a lover of art, gladly consented

and, inspired by God, ordered a paint-
ing of St. Anthony. A few days afterwards, the artist returned, bringing with him a life-sized picture, rep-
resenting the saint with two angels
above his head. In his right hand, he
holds a lily, the symbol of his virginal
purity, and in his left a book, on
which the holy Child is standing. St.
Anthony has a gentle but serious ex-
pression on his countenance, and is
clothed in the habit of the reformed
Tyrolese Province. Under his feet
the spire of the church is seen.
The nobleman, finding he had not
enough money in his purse to pay
the painter, left the room to get some
more. To his great astonishment, on
his return, the painter had disappeared, and, in spite of every inquiry,
was nowhere to be found. This cir-
cumstance has led many to believe

that the picture is the work of an angel, and they are probably right in their conjecture, for it has never been found possible to make a correct copy of it. For two hundred years St. Anthony worked so many miracles at the church at Kattern that it was impossible to inscribe them on the registers, and the walls of his chapel were so covered with *ex votos* from the grateful clients of the saint that the old ones had to make room for the new. It was a common saying: "If St. Anthony will not hear you at Padua, go to Kattern; he is sure to hear you there."

PART III.

PETITIONS GRANTED IN MORE MODERN TIMES.

69.—Saved from Eternal Damnation.

A MAN had for twenty-four years concealed in confession a grievous mortal sin, so that every time he received the sacraments he committed fresh sacrileges. At last a ray of light pierced through his darkened soul, and he implored the assistance of St. Anthony. One day whilst saying his prayers the saint appeared, and so forcibly pointed out to him the infinite justice of God, and the danger of eternal damnation, that, filled with terror, the poor sinner hastened to make a good confession and to be reconciled with God.

70.—St. Anthony Converts an Officer.

The wife of an officer was in great distress about her husband, who whilst serving in the army, had lost his faith. One day, when, in order to bring about his conversion, she was imploring St. Anthony's intercession, she suddenly turned to her little daughter, who was kneeling by her side, and said to her: "You must earnestly ask St. Anthony to make your father find what he has lost."

"What has he lost?" innocently asked the child.

"That you will know one day," replied her mother; "but pray earnestly and do not say anything to father about it."

The child did as she was told. Some time after, the officer wanting to speak to his wife, went to her room, and to his surprise found his little girl kneeling before the statue of St. Anthony, entreating him "to give back what father had lost."

Quite astonished at this, he asked himself: "What can I have lost?" Turning to his wife, he asked her the same question: "Wife, tell me what does the child want St. Anthony to find for me; what have I lost that she is praying for me to recover?"

She made no answer, and he did not press the matter, but in spite of himself the thought haunted him. On June 12th, the eve of the feast of St. Anthony, the officer, finding he could get no peace, again asked his wife what he had lost, and insisted on being answered this time. Looking sadly at him, she said: "Are you prepared to leave me forever?"

"I have never thought of such a thing," was the reply, "but if it were the case, perhaps you would not miss me much, as you are constantly praying in church."

"And yet it must be so, dearest husband," she replied, with tears streaming down her face, "if you do not find what you have lost."

He anxiously asked her: "I entreat you to tell me what I have lost."

The poor woman, weeping bitterly, answered: "What have you lost? Your faith, your mother's faith, and as I do not want to be parted from you for eternity, I implore you to come back to that faith, otherwise you cannot go to heaven."

The officer, without saying another word, silently left her, but the anxious wife could hear him repeating to himself: "The faith, my mother's faith, my wife's faith, my child's faith." And during the night, whilst she was praying for him, he paced up and down his room, saying from time to time the same words: "The faith, my mother's faith."

The next day he again went to her room, and finding her dressed in her best clothes, inquired if it was a holiday. "No," was the reply, "but we are going to keep St. Anthony's feast." "Oh, that saint?" said he, pointing to the statue of St. Anthony, "who finds lost things. Well, thank St. Anthony!" And as his wife looked anxiously into his face, he continued: "Yes, dearest wife, I have found what I had lost. Let us go at once and burn a candle before St. Anthony's altar."

They went to the Franciscan monastery, asked to see a priest, and the officer made his confession and was reconciled to God.

71.—The Heathen Baptized on his Death-bed.

A Jesuit missionary Father, stationed at Madena, in the East Indies, sends us the following account of the conversion of a poor heathen who had often heard the Christians speak of St. Anthony. Whilst still a pagan, he had such devotion to St. Anthony that he used yearly to make a pilgrimage to his altar, and also give a dinner to thirty poor persons in his honor. In spite of this, he did not become a Christian. At last he fell dangerously ill, and, whilst on his sick-bed, remembered his dear St. Anthony. Anxious, as he said, to see him in heaven, he

sent for the Jesuit Father, and asked to
be baptized. The priest, availing himself of the poor man's good dispositions, instructed him in our holy religion, baptized him, gave him the
scapular, and had the consolation of
seeing him die in the best dispositions.

72.—St. Antbony assists Poor Nuns.

Missouri, June 1, 1882.

A teaching order of nuns had been
settled for some time in one of the
large towns of Missouri, but, owing to
the expiration of the lease of the house
in which they resided, they were forced
to look for a place where they could
build a convent. Unfortunately money
was scarce with them. In vain they appealed for assistance; none was forthcoming, and being at an utter loss how
to procure funds sufficient to build

even a convent of the humblest description, they at last thought of placing the matter in St. Anthony's hands, promising him if he did really prove a friend to them, to have it published in the German paper entitled *Sanct Franzisci Glöcklein.*

Their confidence was not misplaced. Funds came from a most unexpected quarter, and they have now not only a more convenient convent for themselves, but also the charge of the parish schools and a high school for American young ladies.

73.—Honor Vindicated.

December 12, 1883.

Whilst staying at a house at ——, which I used frequently to visit, a considerable sum of money was suddenly missed from a room in

which no one else had been but
myself. I could clearly see, though
not openly accused of the theft, that
every one thought I was the guilty
party. Naturally enough, I felt my
position most keenly. To leave my
friend's house would only have confirmed his suspicions, and yet what
was to be done? Nothing was left
but for me to implore assistance from
above, and I determined to make a
novena to St. Anthony, begging of
him to vindicate my honor. On the
third day of the novena the owner of
the lost money suddenly remembered
he had removed it from the place from
which it had been missed, and locked
it up elsewhere. He at once went to
fetch it, and to my great joy found it
perfectly safe. In this way was my
honor vindicated, thanks to that dear
saint.

74.—St. Anthony assists all those Who Invoke him.

Rothsburg, November 18, 1879.

Our present chaplain was taken dangerously ill, and consequently we were without any spiritual assistance. In this emergency we resolved to ask St. Anthony to obtain the cure of our respected pastor, promising at the same time to make a novena of the nine Tuesdays in his honor. We began it on July 15th and on the feast of the Assumption our good priest was well enough to preach to us.

75.—Saved from Drowning.

An Italian priest from Carlovago on the Adriatic sea, writing to the *Sanct Francisci Glöcklein*, begs, out of gratitude, for the following paragraph to be inserted: "On June 24, 1881, I

had to hire a boat to take me to my
parish in order to say Mass. Suddenly
a storm arose and the north wind began to blow with such violence that
the boat began to fill with water.
Death, humanly speaking, was in-
evitable. Bearing, as I do, St. Anthony's name, and having great confidence in his protection, I at once
called upon him to come to our rescue,
and thanks to his powerful assistance
we were saved."

76.—Preserved from Fire.

The following incident took place
in the Tyrol in 1881: A young girl
in the month of March dreamed that
her neighbor's house was on fire, and in
her terror rushed to the window, where
she saw a young Franciscan monk in
the street, who, blessing her house,
said to her father, who was standing

on the doorstep: "Do not be afraid, the fire will not touch you."

This dream made a deep impression on her, and when, the following June, her neighbor's house, just opposite, was struck by lightning during a terrible thunder-storm and burnt to the ground, she at once remembered her dream and St. Anthony's promise. All the time the fire lasted she continually called upon St. Anthony to bless her family and save their house, which he did, for although the roof was thatched and there was a high wind blowing, the fire did not touch it. Truly it can be said: "If you want a miracle go to St. Anthony."

77.—St. Anthony's Protection.

The following account, showing the care Our Lady and St. Anthony take of all who call upon them, is from an

extract of a letter written in thanksgiving by M. S., who lived in the
little town of Pecham, in Austria,
and published in the *Sanct Franzisci
Glöcklein*, dated September 15, 1885:
On May 31st a fire broke out at midnight, completely destroying forty
houses. About one o'clock of the same
night the brother of M. S., who kept
a shop, had the roof of his house burnt,
and all the goods placed in the yard
destroyed. Fearing they would lose
everything, M. S., her brother, and
the other members of the family, im-
prudently rushed back to their sitting-
room, in the hopes of being able to
save a few articles. Owing to the ra-
pidity of the fire and the dense smoke,
they had hardly reached the room before all possibility of exit or rescue
was cut off, and there they were obliged to remain for three hours, ex-

pecting every moment to perish in the flames. M. S. had often read in the *Sanct Franzisci Glöcklein* of the miracles worked by St. Anthony. Full of confidence, she and all those with her fell on their knees, imploring Our Lady of Seven Dolors and St. Anthony to protect them. They were not mistaken, for although the cellar was filled with casks of petroleum and other dangerous combustibles, although all the window sashes were destroyed by the fire, and red hot cinders not only fell into the cellar, but even under the beds, yet not even a single article in the house, except a few sacks of potatoes, were destroyed.

78.—Saved from Shipwreck and Other Difficulties.

In the autumn of 1880 a merchant went with his family to America.

During the voyage they encountered
such stormy weather that even the
oldest sailors on board feared they
were lost. The merchant's wife, a devout client of St. Anthony, promised
if they reached land, not only to make
a pilgrimage to the tomb of St. Anthony, but also that her little girl,
who was being educated in a convent
in Europe, should wear the Franciscan
habit for three months in his honor.
Her prayer was heard, and on her return home she not only visited the
shrine of the saint, but also had a
habit of St. Francis made, which the
child wore for the first time on his
feast, June 13th.

About the end of May, 1881, four
Franciscan monks sailed from New
York for Glasgow, intending to pass
through Edinburgh on their way to
Hull, where they were to take the first

steamer sailing for Rotterdam. To
save expense they had, on reaching
Glasgow, sent their luggage on to
Hull, where, on arriving, to their great
dismay, it was nowhere to be found at
the luggage office. Two of them,
greatly annoyed and quite out of
temper, determined to go and pay a
visit to the Catholic church at some
distance from the port. Their devotions finished, they left the church,
intending to rejoin their fellow
travellers, but found it quite impossible to remember their way back
to the place where they had left
them. In this dilemma they had
recourse to St. Anthony, and not in
vain.

A young man, seeing they were in
trouble and strangers, accosted them,
and after inquiring what was the matter, not only acted as their guide and

brought them back to their companions, but also found the lost luggage,
and never left them till they were safe
on board their vessel.

.

79.—St. Antbony finds Lost People.

Saalem, September 24, 1883.

Some time in September, 1883, a
blind, imbecile, and self-willed old
woman left her home under the pre-
text of going to see some relatives
close by. Finding she did not return
home that night the people of the
house where she lived naturally
concluded she had stayed with her
friends. However, early on the
second day, hearing she had not
been to their house, but had been seen
wandering through some fields, they
became alarmed and people were sent,
but to no purpose, in search of her.

On the third day her relatives had a
Mass said in honor of the Sacred
Hearts of Jesus and Mary, and St. Anthony, with the promise of publishing
it in the *Sanct Franzisci Glöcklein* were
she found, but in spite of inquiries being made in every direction and in the
surrounding villages, they met with no
better success than on the preceding
day. Finally, long after one o'clock
in the afternoon one of the searchers
noticed a lonely path leading into
the woods, where the poor creature,
more dead than alive, was found
sitting under a tree, but so ex-
hausted for want of food, which she
had not tasted for more than two days,
that it was with great difficulty she was
carried home. She is now, thank God,
in perfect health.

80.—A Mistake in Reckoning Discovered.

Cologne, 1884.

A bookkeeper, in balancing his books, found a considerable deficit in them, which he, morally speaking, thought he was in duty bound to make up.

In his difficulty he had recourse to St. Anthony, promising to offer up in the saint's name all the Masses and communions of the month for the intentions of the Church. He once more began carefully to re-examine his books and accounts. After uselessly spending three days in this work, he again called on St. Anthony to assist him, and in a few minutes afterward discovered his mistake.

81.—The Lost Railway Ticket.

Holland, 1885.

A bishop belonging to the Third Order of St. Francis, and a devout client of St. Anthony, had to go on a long journey, and, one day whilst waiting for the train to start, lost his ticket. After searching in vain everywhere for it, he asked St. Anthony to help him, and was just on the point of going to the ticket-office for another when a porter came up to him and said: "Sir, have you lost your ticket? If so, go to the guard, for he has found one, and if it is yours will return it."

82.—The Lost Document.

About forty years ago a convent of nuns in Lower Austria received most extraordinary assistance from St. An-

thony. They were threatened with a
lawsuit, and if on the day of the trial
a certain document was not produced
it would entail the loss of 30,000 florins. The Father Superior, who took
great interest in the Sisters, asked the
Rev. Mother a short time before the
trial began to give him the above-mentioned necessary document, but to her
great dismay she could not find it. At
last she sent for some Sisters to help
her. Every cupboard, shelf and nook
where there was a chance of finding it
were most carefully searched, but to
no purpose. The Father, seeing the
great distress of the Sisters, and
knowing how important it was for
the papers to be found, said to
the Rev. Mother and the few
Sisters who were in the secret;
"There is nothing else to be done but
to ask St. Anthony to help you." The

Rev. Mother at once went with the Sisters to the chapel and, kneeling before the statue of the saint, entreated him to help them. Just as they were leaving the chapel and about to resume their weary task, they met a lay Sister coming down-stairs with a large basket in her arms which she put on the ground near the chapel door, while she rested a moment.

"What have you got there?" said the superioress to the Sister.

"You told me yesterday to clean the attics, Rev. Mother, and as I could not finish them yesterday I have done so to-day."

"What have you in the basket?"

"Broken slates, waste paper and a lot of rubbish."

Whilst this conversation was going on one of the Sisters began examining the waste paper, and all of a sudden

cried out: "Mother, mother, we are
saved; here are the papers," taking
up one of the pieces and handing it
to the superioress. The latter was at
first quite overcome, but, soon recovering herself, said:

"Let us go at once to the chapel
and thank God and St. Anthony;"
then, turning to the lay Sister, "And
you, Sister, go to Father ——— and
tell him the papers are found."

The feelings of the Sisters can be
easily imagined at this marked proof
of the providence of God watching
over them. Had they left the chapel
a minute earlier or later they would
not have met the Sister, and the papers
with the other rubbish would certainly
have been thrown in the dust hole, and
who would have thought of finding
them there? It has never been discovered who put the papers in the attic,

but one thing is certain, that God sent the Sister down-stairs just at the nick of time, thanks to the intercession of St. Anthony.

83.—Clearsighted.

In the year 1841 Dr. Joh. Ness Ringseis, the well-known author and physician of Munich, was invited by the Rev. Father Valentine Riedl, rector of the seminary at Freising, and afterwards bishop of Regensburgh, to go and spend some time with him in this beautiful part of Bavaria, in order to recuperate his health after a dangerous attack of inflammation of the lungs. He availed himself of this enforced rest to complete some valuable manuscripts. On his leaving the seminary, he found he had not sufficient room in his trunk for them, and

asked his friend the sculptor, Conrad
Everard, also on a visit to Freising,
to take them back to his wife
on his return to Munich. This
good lady, anxious to spare her husband, the doctor, all the discomforts of
changing houses, during his absence removed to a larger and more
commodious residence. On his return
home his first thoughts were for his
manuscripts, but although his wife
remembered seeing them, she quite
forgot where they had been put.
Greatly annoyed at this, both husband
and wife began searching all over the
house for the missing papers, but
without success. Ringseis, thinking
that perhaps, after all, his friend had
not sent them to Munich, wrote to the
rector at Freising to inquire if by
chance they were there, but Father
Riedl replied, saying that no such pa-

pers had been seen. On this, the doctor, quite beside himself, rushed to his wife's room without waiting even to finish his letter, to inform her of the bad news. On leaving her he resumed the perusal of his letter, which his friend, knowing he was a sincere Christian, concluded in this way: "Go and ask St. Anthony to help you." Greatly struck by these words, he immediately knelt down, begging the saint's assistance. On returning to his library to continue his search, the first thing that met his eyes was the lost manuscript. Perfectly bewildered with joy, it was some time before he could recover his scattered senses, and then to his surprise found himself sitting on the floor, his loved manuscripts in his lap, large books and folios of the Museum Florentinum strewn round about him. These, he remembered,

owing to their size, had been placed
on the lowest shelf of the library, and
as they reached the next one it was
impossible to see any papers had they
been put behind them. The only conclusion to which he could come was
that the moment he had entered the
room St. Anthony had obtained for
him the gift of clear sight, that is, seeing through opaque objects, which had
enabled him to find his manuscripts.
Some years later Dr. Ringseis became
a tertiary of St. Francis, and was renowned throughout the south of Germany not only for his great learning,
but for his sincere piety.

84.—Founô Again.

A parish priest living at K ——
had paid seventy-seven florins for
a chasuble he had bought in
Holy Week. At the commence-

ment of the following year he received a summons demanding payment for the above-mentioned vestment. Naturally enough, he went to look for the receipt he had received on sending the post-office order. It was nowhere to be found. He searched all over the presbytery, emptied the chest where he kept his books and papers, examined them sheet by sheet, leaf by leaf, but to no purpose. He then went to the post-office, but the money had not been entered in the register. The loss of seventy-seven florins is a serious loss at any time to a priest, and more especially in our days; but great as the loss was it was nothing to be compared with the grief he felt at the thought of his good name being at stake, for to all appearances he had not paid the money, but kept it for

himself. In his distress he mentioned
it to some of his intimate friends, who
tried to console him as best they could,
urging him to pray to St. Anthony,
who would be sure to find it. Comforted a little, he asked them to join
with him in saying the well-known
antiphon, *Si quaeris miracula*, to
which they gladly consented. Greatly
encouraged, the priest returned to his
chest, and calling on St. Anthony to
help him, as he had helped so many
others, took off the lid in order to
empty it more easily. On opening the
box, which was uppermost, the first
thing he found was the missing receipt. He was so overcome that he
began to cry, and then ran to call his
curate, saying: "Pray read this; what
is it?"

"What!" replied the curate, "I con-
gratulate you; it is nothing else but

the paper you have been so long searching for."

"Oh!" exclaimed the poor priest; "if I had only prayed to St. Anthony he would have spared me many sleepless nights."

85.—Seven Hundred Francs Recovered.

The sum of 1200 francs had been stolen from a merchant, Nicholas Raulling von Esh. The police, suspecting a man whom they had noticed had been spending a great deal of money, arrested him, and in spite of his denying the theft he was committed to prison. Many persons, however, believed him innocent, and declared that the man who had been robbed had not so much money in his house. Hearing this, the merchant had recourse to St. Anthony, whose protection he had many times previously experienced, imploring him to return him his money, and, what was still more precious, preserve his good name. A few days afterwards the prisoner sent for his lawyer, acknowledged his guilt, and informed him that he would find the greater part of the money buried in a field. This proved to be perfectly true, and seven hundred francs were returned to their rightful owner.

86.—Money Returned.

Between the night of August 20 and 21, 1884, the sacristy of the church at Neukirchen was broken in, and a safe containing 23,030 marks in paper and one hundred and thirty-two in silver were stolen. Immediately the rector of the church began a novena to the Sacred Hearts of Jesus and Mary, and to

St. Anthony, in order to obtain the recovery of the lost money. The first
day of the novena was not finished before a man from the neighborhood was
seen coming to the presbytery carrying the stolen safe, in which the lost
money was found untouched. Let those
who are in difficulties or affliction have
recourse to the Sacred Hearts of Jesus
and Mary and to St. Anthony; they
will be sure to find help.

87.—The Valuable Sketch.

Innsbruck, January 16, 1884.

A friend of mine had a sketch of
Our Lady drawn by an unknown
artist, and intended to have a copy of
it made on glass. The sketch in itself
was very beautiful, and a connoisseur
declared it was long time since he had
seen anything to equal it. All of a

sudden it was missed. The house was searched from top to bottom, every cupboard, chest of drawers, desk, were emptied, but to no purpose. Inquiries were even made to discover whether it had slipped into a collection of drawings which had been sent away. Useless trouble. One day my friend happened to speak to me about his loss, and promised he would have it made into a picture for an altar in my church if it were ever found. I was now an interested party, and I begged of him, together with another priest, to join with me in making a novena to St. Anthony of Padua. That dear saint has on many occasions proved himself a good friend to me, and I felt certain he would be so again. The novena was finished. A week, a month passed, but still no picture. I have just received a letter to-day from my friend. The sketch is found. One day one of the maid servants, finding it lying about, thought it was of no value, and had coolly taken it and nailed it to the wall in her room.

88.—From Caffraria.

Under the burning sun of South Africa, even as in the old country, this dear saint is ever quite as ready to help his clients to recover lost articles.

Five Sisters of the Holy Cross from Messingen, Switzerland, had been sent to teach the Christians and heathens in Umtata, a small town in Caffraria. A farm provided them with the bare necessaries of life. In spite of this, their life was one of continual self-sacrifice.

One morning not less than six oxen, a cow and her calf were missing.

Impossible to find them. A great
cross certainly for our poor mission-
aries. St. Anthony was stormed; he
was in duty bound to advise and assist
the Sisters, and, of course, he did so.
The head steward of the farm remembered he had been obliged to dis-
charge a Caffre servant for his laziness
and unpunctuality. The characteristic
feature of the Caffre is revenge, and
no doubt the one just dismissed had
driven the cattle away during the
night. His track was discovered, but
all private search proved useless. At
last the matter was placed in the
hands of a magistrate, and at the end
of ten days the police found the animals, half-starved, in the possession
of the Caffre, who was condemned not
only to restore the stolen property, but
also to give one of his own cows and
her calf as a compensation to the

rightful owners. From this time not only did the devotion to St. Anthony become dearer to the Sisters, but it has spread all over this part of the country.

89.—The Stolen Watch.

June 10, 1884.

During a short absence from my room my watch was stolen. On my giving information of it to the police, it was discovered that just at that time an ex-convict had been seen loafing about the street near my house. He was arrested, but declared he had not taken it, and as my watch was not found on his person, set free. Human means having failed, I had recourse to St. Anthony, promising to have his antiphon said at the Mass in his honor. A few days afterwards, just before the church was going to be

locked up for the night, a woman who
was praying unnoticed near one of the
chapels saw the same man go straight
to the altar, put something on it, and
then leave the church. The sacristan,
on being told what had happened, at
once went to the altar, and, on opening the parcel and finding it was my
watch, immediately came and brought
it back to me. Heartfelt thanks to the
great thaumaturgus.

90.—"See, the Watch is Found!"

One Sunday morning after High
Mass, in spite of the repeated remon-
strances of my confessor about my
working on Sundays, I finished mend-
ing a valuable watch which was to be
called for that afternoon, and then left
it lying on the table, with several
others, in my workshop. It may have

been mere accident or a punishment from God, but on my coming back some time later to my shop the watch had disappeared. I looked everywhere for it; impossible to find it. I went to the police. The children who had been playing in the house with mine were searched; the thief could not be found. I even offered to give a person whom I had every reason to suspect, but dared not openly accuse of theft, a new watch or money if he would only give the other one back to me. This he refused, saying he had never seen the watch. What my feelings were can be easily imagined. Had the watch been my own the loss would have been bad enough; but, being the property of another, my reputation for honesty was at stake, which made matters ten thousand times worse.

Some kind friends, hearing of my misfortune, came to see me and advised me to have recourse to St. Anthony, for said they: "This good saint is certain to find the watch for you, even if he has to make the thief return it." I at once acquiesced to their proposal, and we immediately began to say three Our Fathers in his honor three times a day. This was continued for a week, my trust in the powerful intercession of St. Anthony daily increasing. On Sunday during High Mass I felt sure the watch would be found, although there seemed to be no signs of it. On Monday afternoon I went to help the man who was working in my field, taking my wife and children with me, so that no one was left at home. At two o'clock my wife went back to the house, and, on going to the place close to the window where the latch-key was hidden, noticed something wrapped up in paper. What was her surprise on undoing the paper to find the lost watch. She ran breathless back to me, crying out: "St. Anthony has helped us; the watch is found."

91.—St. Anthony is Ever Ready to Assist.

Wonderful are God's workings in His saints, but more especially in the manner He makes use of St. Anthony to relieve and assist those who in their difficulties or trials have recourse to the intercession of His faithful servant. It is in order to encourage others to place their trust in this universal favorite that I am going to relate one or two things which happened to myself.

During the French war in 1870 I was sent with other Brothers to nurse

the sick and wounded in France. On
Christmas eve we reached the little
town of Corbeille, on the Seine, where,
for want of better accommodation, we
had, together with members of other
orders, to take up our sleeping quar-
ters in the Hotel de Ville. I cannot
wish for a better picture of the stable
at Bethlehem. A few bundles of
straw on a stone floor served us for
beds. Owing to most of the windows
being broken, there were draughts on
every side. Impossible to light a fire
in the stove for want of fuel. It was
a consolation for us to think that on
that Christmas night we shared the
sufferings and discomforts of the holy
Child at Bethlehem. We rose early
next morning in order to say Mass at
a convent at some distance. Our
Brothers were soon ready to start, except one, whom I noticed was anx-

iously searching for something in the straw. I asked him what was the matter. On being told he had lost the key of our valise, I at once said a "Hail Mary" in honor of St. Anthony. It was not finished before I felt myself as if pushed down on the ground. I put my hand in the straw in which our brother had been searching for the key and at once found it. Glory be to God in the highest, and honor to St. Anthony, to whom God has given such power.

Another time, again on Christmas eve, 1884, I wanted to read over a manuscript I had just finished. For more than half an hour I searched every sheet of paper lying on my table one by one; impossible to find the paper I wanted. Meeting one of our Brothers, I told him my loss. "Have you prayed to St. Anthony?" he asked.

I had quite forgotten to do so, and, on being thus reminded, immediately went to the chapel and said a prayer to the dear saint. Returning to my cell, I at once resumed my search, and was about giving it up as useless when I heard an interior voice distinctly say to me I would find the lost manuscript under the other papers, which proved to be the case. I am now convinced that God permitted my having so much trouble in finding the manuscript in order for me to honor and have greater confidence in dear St. Anthony.

92.—Striking Combination of Circumstances.

I was engaged as geometrician to take the measurement of a small fish pond which was to be let on lease. Not suspecting there was another close by,

I naturally went to the first one which came in my sight. Whilst taking the necessary instruments for my work I missed a small and valuable one called a geometric pen. For more than an hour my two assistants, myself and three boys searched all over the grass near the pond in the hopes of finding it. At last we said a rosary for the souls in purgatory, and after praying to St. Anthony I promised to have a Mass said in his honor. I then resumed my work and on finishing it, seeing a man coming from the other side of the pond, near which there was a nursery of young trees, entered into conversation with him. I soon discovered there was a pond in the middle of the trees and that this was the one to be let. Of course, I went to fetch my instruments, but hardly had I taken two steps before I saw the identical lost pen lying on the ground. I could not help thinking to myself how extraordinary the ways of God are, for had I not met the man, not only would I have measured the wrong pond, but also not found the lost pen.

93.—Pilgrimage to St. Antbony's Cburcb at Oberacbern.

About 1765 the inhabitants of Ober-achern, in the Grand Duchy of Baden, and the inhabitants of the neighboring villages built a magnificent church in the place of the old wooden chapel, erected on the very spot where some pigs had discovered and dug up the miraculous statue of St. Anthony. In 1770 a picture commemorating this extraordinary event was laid on the tomb of St. Anthony at Padua, and after remaining there three days was blessed and sent back to the church at Oberachern. To inquiries which had been made respecting the pilgrimage to Oberachern, the following answer was given: "This spot is undoubtedly a favored one, for Masses are constantly asked to be said here, either for the pilgrims themselves, or for others anxious to be restored to health or obtain other graces through the intercession of St. Anthony. The Church is now covered with *ex votos*, and fresh miracles are constantly taking place." We shall only speak about one which took place in 1880. That year Madame von Urloffen, a lady well known in the Duchy of Baden, wrote and asked the rector of the Church of St. Anthony to have a Mass said in honor of the saint for her intention.

Her son, a boy of twelve, was acci-

dentally shot in the eye, and it was so
seriously injured that, acting on the
advice of the physicians of their own
town, he was taken to the eye infirmary at Freiburg and placed under
the care of the celebrated oculist, Pro-
fessor Manz, who, after a careful ex-
amination of the diseased eye, declared
it was beyond medical skill to cure it,
and strongly advised it to be cut out.
To this Madame von Urloffen was
greatly averse, and entreated the doctor, unless her son's life was in im-
mediate danger, to postpone the operation for a fortnight. On his con-
senting to it, mother and son began
earnestly to implore the assistance of
St. Anthony, since human science was
of no avail. The saint heard their
petition. In a few days the eye was
decidedly improved, and when at the
end of a fortnight the boy was taken

to the infirmary the doctor, on seeing him, exclaimed: "This is a miracle; there is no longer any necessity for an operation." The child has now perfectly recovered his eyesight, and has since made a pilgrimage in thanksgiving to the church at Oberachern, accompanied by his mother.

94.—Sickness Yields to the Intercession of St. Anthony of Padua.

Although I have had the happiness of being a tertiary of the Third Order of St. Francis of Assisi for some years, I knew very little about the life of St. Anthony of Padua till a friend of mine brought me the life and account of the miracles of this great saint, by Father Philibert Seebock. Since reading it I have always felt so great devotion and confidence in St.

Anthony that I have never missed saying the antiphons in his honor, and,
oh, how promptly and generously has
he rewarded me! Not long ago my
dear mother, already advanced in
years, fell dangerously ill, and seeing
her sufferings increase, I at once had
recourse to the intercession of this
good saint, entreating him to obtain
from the Sacred Heart the cure of
that beloved parent. I also promised
to begin a novena of nine holy communions, say the litany and antiphon
in his honor, and have an account
of her cure published in the *Sanct
Franczisci Glöcklein*. I had scarcely
finished my prayers before my mother
called out to me, saying, "God be
praised, I feel better. The pain is not
so acute. I think I shall get well."
She is now perfectly recovered from
her illness, although, of course, a little

weak. A thousand thanks to the Sacred Heart, who has granted me this blessing through the intercession of His great miracle worker.

95.—¶ncontestable Miracle.

The following wonderful cure of a Sister of Charity, which took place June 13, 1886, is extracted from an account sent to the *Osservatore Catolico.* Her sisters, after doing all in their power to save the life of their dear invalid, determined to have recourse to St. Anthony, and every one began, in order to prepare herself for his feast, by making a tridicini, or thirteen days' prayer, in his honor, for this intention. On the morning of his feast Sister Olive was perfectly cured.

The following is an account of her

illness, written by Dr. Chemin, the director of the hospital at Bassano, to the very Reverend Mother General of the Order.

VERY REV. MOTHER GENERAL :

It is my duty to inform you of a most extraordinary and consoling event which has just taken place here at Bassano. I mean the sudden cure of Sister Olive, who was literally at death's door. Late in the evening of Saturday, June 12th, I visited her professionally, and found her suffering greatly, being unable to get her breath, owing to dropsy, which had increased so greatly that it was impossible to perceive the upheavings of the chest. I considered death so imminent that I wrote to my friend, the director of the hospital at Rovigno, about the kind of grave which was to be prepared for a Sister of Charity.

At four o'clock on Sunday morning. June 13th, Sister Olive got out of bed, a thing she had not done for two months, went to the room of the Sister Superior and awoke her, saying "I am cured." The good Sister, thinking she was delirious, sent her back to bed. At eight o'clock I returned to the hospital to make my usual visits, and what was my surprise, on entering the part assigned to the Sisters of Charity, to see my patient up and dressed. As soon as I recovered from my astonishment, I carefully examined her, but could find no trace of disease. This incontestable cure cannot be scientifically accounted for, it is so far beyond the reach of the natural order of things. Not only had I given up every hope of curing her, but the two physicians who attended her conjointly with myself were of the same opinion, and such being the case, it is sufficient matter for the reflection of the materialists. Sister Olive continues so well that yesterday she was able to receive holy communion in the church. In one word, it could be nothing else but a miracle.

I remain, very Rev. Mother General, yours, etc.,

Dr. F. Chemin.

Bassano, June 16, 1869.

96.—Praise be to God and his holy servant Anthony.

Innsbruck, June 20, 1885.

"For three years I suffered greatly from general debility, which rendered me perfectly incapable of any exertion. During the last six months of my illness my circumstances were so changed that it became imperative for me to earn my livelihood, and a situation was found for me. As every earthly means of curing me had failed, I had recourse to the assistance of One who is ever ready to help those who implore His intercession. I promised to enter the Third Order of St. Francis of Assisi, and began a novena for this intention. On the second day of the novena I already found myself better, and before it was ended was perfectly cured. I have now an excellent appetite, sleep well, which was never the case before, have entered my situation, and can endure any amount of fatigue."

97.—Prompt Assistance.

Innsbruck, February 2, 1882.
"We shall be grateful to the editor of the *Sanct Franczisci Glöcklein,* if he

will kindly insert in his valuable paper,
the enclosed, among the long list of
favors St. Anthony bestows on those
who ask his intercession.

"The father of a respectable family,
in the prime of life, had suffered for
some months from general debility,
which made one suspect the existence
of an internal complaint. The physician who sounded him thought the
seat of the disease lay in the lungs,
which was confirmed by the continual
pain he had near that region. His
poor wife, seeing him daily wasting
away, did nothing but weep. At
last a friend, touched by the intensity
of her grief, advised her to make a
novena to St. Anthony, which she at
once began, and promised to make
the novena of the nine Tuesdays
should her dear husband be restored to
health. Scarcely was the first novena

ended before a marked improvement
was noticed in the patient, his appetite returned, he slept well, and before
the second novena was finished he had
perfectly recovered."

98.—Paralysis Cured.

Claudia Bartolini, a young woman
of nineteen, residing with her parents
at 6 Via delle Penzochere, Florence,
had, owing to a severe attack of gout,
become perfectly paralyzed on the left
side, and could only crawl about on
crutches. Every possible remedy had
been tried in vain. At last a rich and
pious lady took her in hand, and
placed her under the care of the good
Passionist nuns, who encouraged her
to have recourse to St. Anthony.
This year the good nuns had her
carried to the large and beautiful

Church of Santa Croce, where the
saint's feast was to be celebrated
with great pomp and solemnity. Here
she must have prayed with great devotion, for in the middle of the Mass,
in presence of an immense congregation, she suddenly stood up, threw
away her crutches and exclaimed :
" I am cured." The authenticity of
this miracle has been officially signed
by the episcopal authorities of Florence.

99.—A Needle Swallowed.

The Rev. Capuchin Father P. W.,
residing in A——, guarantees the
veracity of the following incident,
which happened to one of his parishioners, Mrs. F. H.

On the 14th of November, 1893, she
swallowed a needle, which was con-

cealed in some food. She never suspected what it was, but thought it
might be a sharp bit of bone which
pricked her so much. From that time
on she suffered great pain, especially
when drinking, and this, during an
attack of influenza, owing to the great
thirst she experienced, increased
greatly. The doctors tried in vain to
pull the supposed bone out of her
throat, but only drove the needle in
further. The poor sufferer constantly implored St. Anthony to relieve
her. It was not in vain, for on the
25th of November, while clearing her
throat, she felt something move up,
and, putting at once her two fingers
in her mouth, pulled up, to her great
astonishment, a large needle.

100.—St. Anthony Bestows the Gift of Medical Penetration.

November 1, 1880.

As parish priest I have not only myself frequently experienced the assistance of St. Anthony in serious cases, but have constantly urged my parishioners to invoke him in every emergency. To-day I shall confine myself to speak about a case which recently happened, and which proves how ready he is to help those who invoke his intercession. At the commencement of this month I was called to visit a sick man, suffering from acute pains in the bowels. Danger of death seemed imminent, and I administered the last sacraments to him, encouraging him at the same time to place great confidence in the intercession of St. Anthony. I told him I would copy out the antiphons of the saint for him, and bring them with me on my next visit. This I did. On my return to the sick man, he declared the pain had become so unbearable that the doctors feared inflammation had set in. After listening to all he had to say to me, I read the antiphons to him, and made him promise not only that he would say them every day, but if he recovered he would join the Third Order of St. Francis of Assisi.

When I was once more in my study I mechanically took up a medical book which was lying on my table, and in distraction began turning over the pages. Suddenly my eye caught the passage speaking about the treatment of persons suffering from worms. I read the page carefully over, and the thought at once struck me that my poor parishioner might be suffering from them. I immediately went to see him, and, after carefully questioning him, felt convinced I was not mistaken in my surmises. I made him take some worm powders, which effectually destroyed the enemy. He is now perfectly cured and has joined the Third Order, as promised.

Knowing the interest you take in everything tending to promote the devotion to St. Anthony, I am certain you will publish the above-mentioned cure in the *Sanct Franzisci Glöcklein,* as it may be an encouragement for others to apply to this dear saint in an emergency.

101.—Swelling of the Throat Cured.

Dear Mr. Editor: I think it is my duty to inform you of the miraculous

manner in which St. Anthony has just
cured me of a bad swelling in my
throat, which was rapidly increasing—
medical assistance being of no avail.
I am not only a subscriber of the *Sanct
Franzisci Glöcklein*, but also a member of the Third Order of St. Francis
of Assisi. The perusal of the many
favors obtained through the intercession of St. Anthony, which are
published monthly, encouraged me to
make a novena to St. Anthony and to
ask you to insert it in the *Sanct Franzisci Glöcklein*, so that my brothers and
sisters of the Third Order might be
induced to have recourse to this dear
Father. On the second day of the
novena, I noticed that the swelling in
my throat had considerably decreased,
and before the novena was half over
it had completely disappeared. (Extract taken from a letter written to the

editor of the *Sanct Franzisci Glöcklein,*
November 30, 1881.)

102.—Ibow St. Antbon\̇y listens to Ibis Clients.

A nun had already received the last
.acraments and lay in the agonies of
death. Her father, well aware of the
tender-heartedness of Father Colnago,
S.J., implored him to go and visit his
sick daughter. On reaching the
convent, the reverend Father at
once went to the grille, and
said to one of the nuns : " Do
you want your invalid cured ? "
" Certainly, Father, " replied the religious, hardly able to conceal a smile.
"Well, then," said the Jesuit, "we
will cure her; we have only to ask St.
Anthony." Then raising his eyes
up to heaven, he made the sign of the
cross three times over a rosary,

and ordered the nun to take it to her dying sister, Johanna Tedeschi. Hardly had the sick nun touched the rosary before she was completely cured.

103.—The Signet Ring.

One day a patient of Dr. M., noticing he was not in his usual spirits, but quite out of temper, wanted to know what was the matter. " What is the matter?" replied the doctor, curtly. "Why, I have just lost a valuable ring; and, after hunting all over the house for it, cannot find it."

"Have you prayed to St. Anthony?" asked the invalid.

"Prayed to whom? To St. Anthony?" said the doctor, scarcely able to suppress a smile of contempt.

"Well, then," answered the lady,

"since you have no confidence in our good St. Anthony, I suppose I must myself ask him to give you back your ring; he is sure to do so." The next day, when he came to pay his usual visit to his patient, her door was hardly open before he laughingly stretched out his hand, with the lost ring on his finger, no longer a disbeliever. He related how the ring had been found in a place he would never have dreamt of searching for it. It appears that morning he had been to see his horse in the stable, and, after staying there some minutes, went away. One of his servants, shortly after he had left, went for something in the stable, and what did she see lying on a heap of manure but the lost ring!

"And now do you believe in my good saint?" asked the fervent client of St. Anthony.

"Well, I suppose I must believe in him this time," laughingly replied the doctor.

104.—The Wedding Ring.

The wife of a baker had lost her wedding ring shortly after her marriage. This greatly vexed her, as it was considered an ill-omen. She earnestly prayed to St. Anthony in the hopes of finding it, but he seemed to have turned a deaf ear to all her entreaties. After searching everywhere for it, she came to the conclusion that she must have lost it while bathing in the Rhine at Breesach, and, therefore, gave up every hope of finding it again. A year had just passed, when the baker's little nephew came to pay them a visit, and one day while bathing in the Rhine, he began poking about the stones in the river, when suddenly something bright attracted his attention. It was the lost ring.

The joy and gratitude of its owner can be easily imagined.

105.—The Thread in the Water.

August 6, 1880.

A poor woman, a tertiary of St. Francis, was dragging a small cask laden with thread up a steep hill, when it accidentally upset, and the whole of its contents rolled into the Agerflusse, a stream in upper Austria. As the thread was her sole means of earning a living, she naturally felt greatly distressed, and at once promised to make a novena to St. Anthony, being certain he would assist her. The following week, as she was passing by the same spot, a workman who was hauling some logs of wood out of the water caught hold of the sack of thread. On the sack being opened, the thread was found none the worse for having been a week in the water.

106.—Three Examples of Lost Money Found.

On June 3, 1879, the porter of a hotel in Montabaur (Nassau), whilst going to Hadamar for a load of fruit, lost a pocketbook containing sixty marks (about twenty dollars), which got him into a great deal of trouble. He at once applied to St. Anthony, promising, if help was forthcoming, to have it published in two newspapers, and also to say two Rosaries in thanksgiving. On his way back from Hadamar the lost pocketbook was handed over to him.

R. Having read in the *Noth-burga* how St. Anthony had assisted a porter in recovering lost money, I determined to try the saint's power, and, thanks to him, I have found the one hundred and fifty francs I had lost.

M. D. I had lost something of no intrinsic value, but which I greatly prized. After searching everywhere I said to myself, "Suppose I say three Our Fathers in honor of St. Anthony; he is sure to find it for me," and I was not mistaken.

107.—Trust and Hope.

Zweibrücken, November 9, 1880.

A farmer, not very well off in the goods of this world, lost a sum of money, the want of which was greatly felt by his family. He at once asked the assistance of St. Anthony, feeling certain that he would help him, and he was not deceived, for a few days afterwards the money was found, and in a place no one would have thought of looking for it. The good man, out of gratitude to God for hearing the prayer of His saint, intends giving, by installments, the same amount of money to erect an altar of the Sacred Heart in the church of that place.

108.—St. Anthony's Assistance.

On July 26, 1879, I noticed, on returning home from a walk, that I had lost a gold locket which I prized very much, not only on account of it having been blessed, but also for its contents. The loss of it did not affect me very much, as St. Anthony never failed helping me in similar circum-

stances. After saying three Our Fathers, and promising to have it published in the *Nothburga*, I retired
to rest as soon as I had finished my prayers. Of course I did not
leave the work of finding the locket to
St. Anthony without taking the
trouble to try and find it myself; but
the next morning I began to visit the
different places to which I had been
the evening before. I was interrupted
in my search by the bell ringing for
Mass. At first I hesitated about going
to church, but finally I made up my
mind to go, for is not one Mass worth
more than all the lockets in the
world? Besides, was there any cer-
tainty of my finding the locket even if
I stayed away? When Mass was over
I continued my walk, but to no purpose. Fearing the trinket might have
fallen into the hands of some one who

would only have cared for its intrinsic value, and perhaps laughed at its contents, I asked Our Lady not to permit such a thing to happen, and for this intention invoked our saintly Father, Pope Pius IX., St. Anne, St. Joachim, and especially St. Anthony, in whose honor I said another Our Father.

I suppose my persistency must have touched our good St. Anthony, for very shortly afterwards a stranger, noticing I was searching for something, accosted me, asking if I had lost anything. On my replying in the affirmative, and giving him a description of my locket, he returned it to me, saying he had found it near St. Mary's Church.

Many thanks to our dear Lady and good St. Anthony and my other holy friends.

109.—The Lost Washing Found.

From Silesia: There is a farm-house at F———, where devotion to St. Anthony is quite a matter of course. He is a member of the family, and naturally his feast is a day of rejoicing.

Master and mistress, children and servants, all go to make their devotions in his church and hear Mass in his honor. St. Anthony is quite at home here, and is constantly showing his loving care for each member of the house.

One morning the milkmaid rose very early to take the milk to town, and as she had the clothes to wash at the public wash house, she put a large bundle of dirty linen in her cart, in order not to have to return home before she had finished her work. A thief, availing himself of the

darkness of the morning, stole
the bundle out of the cart while
she was serving the milk to
her customers. The terror of the
poor girl, on discovering her loss, can
be easily imagined. Her first care was
to give information to the police; her
next, to go and have a Mass said in
honor of St. Anthony, at the Franciscan church. Of course, she naturally expected a good scolding on her
return home, but, to her great astonishment, her mistress, who had already heard of the loss, uttered no
word of reproach and only mingled
her tears with her maid's. When the
farmer came home he gently asked
the women if it was about the lost
linen they were crying. Upon their
answering it was, he said very simply:
"Why do you cry about it? Did not
God give it to us? and if He has al-

lowed it to be taken from us, He can let us have it back again, and besides, there is St. Anthony to help us."

Here let us pause for a moment to consider how much holy trust elevates a soul. This confidence did not remain unrewarded. The very same day a poor widow came to the farm, and said the master and servant girl were to go to the police station, for the linen was found.

This is how it all happened. That very morning the widow had given all her earnings to her children to buy potatoes; it was very little, only four kreuzers (about seven cents). Little as it was, she was very happy. Often she had not so much, and then all she could do was to pray to God to help her. If she only had two kreuzers more, the children might have had a little salt, which would have been a real treat; but God was watching over her, and help was at hand. "Mother," said her eldest boy, "I will go and pick up the bits of broken glass in the canal, and perhaps I shall be able to get a little salt in exchange." He went and saw something lying under the water close to the edge of the canal. Not knowing what to do, he ran home to his mother, who immediately returned with him, and pulled out the bundle of linen. Thinking it might have been stolen, the good widow at once took the bundle to the police station. The police, after examining it, finding it corresponded to the description given by the servant girl, returned it to its rightful owners. As for the poor woman, she was rewarded by the farmer, and is now employed in the house.

One word in conclusion. On comparing the time in which the linen was found, it was discovered it must have been during the elevation of the Mass said in honor of St. Anthony. Honor, praise and glory to God and to his dear St. Anthony.

It may not be out of place to remind you, dear reader, that much as St. Anthony loves to help you in your temporal concerns, he has your spiritual welfare still more at heart. Remember, it was owing to his thirst after the greater glory of God and salvation for souls that he became the instrument chosen by divine Providence to work out the salvation of thousands of poor sinners, to make thousands of heretics renounce their errors and to open the gates of heaven to thousands of the timid and afflicted. It was this great love that induced him to leave Lisbon and then Coimbra, to the astonishment of all, and enter the order of the Friars Minor. He had hoped to go and preach the Gospel to the poor heathen; but God had ordained otherwise, and the vessel on which he sailed for Africa was driven to the coast of Messina. Here he heard St. Francis was holding a General Chapter at Assisi, and thither he hastened to throw himself at the feet of his beloved founder. St. Francis soon discovered the priceless treasure God had sent him in the person of the young and humble monk, who was soon to become one of the greatest champions of the Church. On leaving Assisi St. Anthony preached at Rome, where Pope Gregory IX. surnamed him the "Ark of the Covenant," and the "Hammer of the Heretic," on account of his success with sinners and heretics, as we have already seen.

The children in Padua, on hearing of his death, June 13, 1231, filled the streets with the noise of their lamentations, crying out, " The saint is dead; the saint is dead." More than six hundred years have elapsed since he left this world to receive his reward in heaven, but he still loves souls as dearly as when he lived on earth. Let us, therefore, never fail, in all our difficulties, to invoke one whose life can be summed up in these few words: "Love of God; zeal for His honor; care for the salvation of souls; obedience, humility and patience."

PART IV.

DEVOTIONS AND PRAYERS TO ST. ANTHONY.

110.—The Antiphons of St. Anthony in the Form of Prayer.

O ALMIGHTY and all powerful God! I, the most wretched and unworthy of Thy creatures, prostrate before the throne of Thy infinite mercy, return Thee my most humble thanks for all the graces and power it hath pleased Thee to bestow on Thy saints, but more especially for those lavished on Thy servant Anthony, my dear patron, at whose voice the sick are restored to health, the blind see; the maimed recover their lost limbs; the prisoner his liberty; those in danger at sea are saved from shipwreck; lost friends and things are found; the wretched are consoled; misery of every description relieved; heresy overcome, and even death and hell obey his commands. And this not only in his own city of Padua, but throughout the whole Catholic world.

I, therefore, oh, Almighty God, Father, Son and Holy Ghost! desire to thank Thee for all Thy mercies and goodness and to beseech of Thee to hear and grant my petition in this, my present and all my other necessities, through the intercession and merits of Thy servant, Anthony.

Dear St. Anthony, obtain this favor for me by thy most powerful prayers. Amen.

111.—Prayers for Every Day of the Nine Tuesdays in Honor of St. Anthony.

LITTLE OFFICE OF ST. ANTHONY.

At Matins.

I will praise Thee, O God, in St. Anthony, whose tongue never ceased to praise Thee and to incite others to praise and exalt Thee.

V. O Lord, open my lips.

R. And my mouth shall announce Thy praise.

V. O God, incline unto my aid.

R. O Lord, make haste to help me.

Glory be to the Father, and to the Son, and to the Holy Ghost.

As it was in the beginning, is now, and ever shall be, world without end. Amen.

Hymn.

Hail, St. Anthony! each creature
　Hails thee holy, knows thee great.
In thy childhood, God, thy teacher,
　Drew thy heart to consecrate
All to Him the life then dawning;
　Heavenward set thy little feet;
Worldly pleasures, saint-like scorn-
　　　ing;
　Giving Him thy heart complete.
And sweet Mary, pure and tender,
　Jesus' Mother was thine too;
She became thy strong defender;
　Hers the aid that kept thee true.

Antiphon. In Anthony was from
youth up all grace of the way and of
the truth, all hope of life and of virtue. (Ecclus. xxiv.)

V. The just shall flourish like the
lily.

R. And shall grow up before the Lord.

Prayer.

Grant me, O Lord Jesus Christ, through the delight which Thou hadst together with Thy blessed Virgin Mother, in the innocent life of St. Anthony, to have contrition for the sins of my youth, and vouchsafe me the grace of a true conversion. Who livest and reignest world without end. Amen.

At Lauds.

I will praise Thee, O God, in St. Anthony, whose tongue never ceased to praise Thee and to incite others to praise and exalt Thee.

V. O God, incline unto my aid.

R. O Lord, make haste to help me.

Glory be to the Father, etc.

Hymn.

Let all Christian tongues uniting,
  Greet the hero, brave and calm,
For the faith, undaunted, fighting,
  Meriting the martyr's palm.
See him now, true son of Francis,
  With his spirit all aflame,
Moslem ears his voice entrances,
  Glad to die a crown to claim.
Yet when God forbade this glory,
  Willingly resigned his crown,
Telling Christian ears the story,
  Error shrinking at his frown.

Antiphon. Who will give me wings like a dove, that I fly and follow the footsteps of Jesus Christ Who suffered for us, leaving us an example. (Ps. liv.; 1 Pet. ii.)

V. This is Anthony, whom Jesus loved.

R. So I will have him remain till I come. (John xxi.)

Prayer.

Regard, O God, St. Anthony's great zeal, inflamed with which he desired to shed his blood for love of Thee. Excite in me, too, the desire of proving myself grateful for Thy sacred Passion by a truly Christian life pleasing to Thee. Who livest and reignest world without end. Amen.

At Prime.

I will praise Thee, O God, in St. Anthony, whose tongue never ceased to praise Thee and to incite others to praise and exalt Thee.

V. O God, incline unto my aid.

R. O Lord, make haste to help me.

Glory be to the Father, etc.

Hymn.

Who, ah, who, shall not aspire
  Thee to praise, St. Anthony?
Highest wisdom still grew higher,
  Richer for enriching thee.
Deep humility grew deeper,
  Virtue's blossoms brighter hued,
That thy soul was made their keeper,
  In thy silent solitude,
Till the cross of Christ that claimed
      thee
  Taught thee what no man e'er saw;
"High priest of the Ark" they named
      thee,
  Covenant of Christ's new law.

Antiphon. Behold I have given My
words in thy mouth: lo, I have set thee
this day over the nations, and over
kingdoms, to root up and to pull down,
to build and to plant.   (Jer. i.)

V. I have exalted one chosen out of My people.

R. And My hand shall help him. (Ps. lxxxviii.)

Prayer.

Almighty and eternal God, Who dost regard and graciously hear in heaven the humble of heart: grant us to extirpate the spirit of pride and to please Thy divine sight with true humility of heart. Who livest and reignest world without end. Amen.

At Tierce.

I will praise Thee, O God, in St. Anthony, whose tongue never ceased to praise Thee and to incite others to praise and exalt Thee.

V. O God, incline unto my aid.

R. O Lord, make haste to help me.

Glory be to the Father, etc.

Hymn.

Hail to thee in times unnumbered,
  Spotless lily, white as snow:
In thy soul's fair chalice slumbered
  Balm for healing human woe.
For, sweet Anthony, thy pleading,
  Like an unction, souls to win,
Melted hearts too long unheeding,
  Made the hardest weep for sin.
Speak to us, thy mercy claiming;
  Speak one little word to me;
That the love of God, inflaming,
  Warm our hearts eternally.

V. We have heard him speak.

R. In our own tongues the wonderful works of God.   (Acts ii.)

Prayer.

O God, Who didst in a special manner sanctify and enlighten with the grace of the Holy Ghost the heart of St. Anthony: grant us in the same

Spirit to do all things that are right, and always to rejoice in His divine consolation. Through Jesus Christ Our Lord. Amen.

At Sext.

I will praise Thee, O God, in St. Anthony, whose tongue never ceased to praise Thee and to incite others to praise and exalt Thee.

V. O God, incline unto my aid.

R. O Lord, make haste to help me.

Glory be to the Father, etc.

Hymn.

Be thou praised with heart and voices,
  Saint, so worthy of our task!
Surest wisdom, that rejoices,
  Thou dost bring to those that ask.
What is lost, what gone and vanished,
  What the dark has hid away,
By thy help, when hope is banished,
  God will bring to light of day.

Thou canst, by thy interceding,
  Bind the evil one, and death;
Sickness, danger, doubt misleading,
  All must fly before thy breath.

Antiphon. Come let us go to him who seeth the things that are hidden; for this is truly the finger of God, and his name is wonderful. (Exod. viii.)

V. God has made His holy one wonderful.

R. The Lord will hear me when I shall cry unto Him. (Ps. iv.)

Prayer.

O God, Who showest Thyself most wonderful in St. Anthony, and hast made him illustrious by the continual splendor of miracles: graciously vouchsafe that we may receive through his intercession whatsoever we confidingly implore through his merits. Who

livest and reignest world without end.
Amen.

At None.

I will praise Thee, O God, in St.
Anthony, whose tongue never ceased
to praise Thee and to incite others to
praise and exalt Thee.

V. O God, incline unto my aid.
R. O Lord, make haste to help me.
Glory be to the Father, etc.

Hymn.

All my heart to thee is bended,
    Christ's beloved; great thy part!
God-made Child thou kissed, and
       tended,
    Held so warm against thy heart.
Oh, how tenderly, how sweetly,
    Smiled that little Child on thee!
Bringing gifts He showered metely,
    Great thy worth, and given free.

Gave thee saintly will and power.

Strength to work for heaven's bliss;
He, the Lord, was then thy dower,

More He could not give than this.

Antiphon. My beloved to me and I to him, who feedeth among the lilies. His left hand is under my head, and his right hand shall embrace me. (Cant. ii.)

V. I will not let thee go.

R. Except thou bless me. (Gen. xxxii.)

Prayer.

Reminding thee of thy joy at the apparition of the Infant Jesus, I implore thee, St. Anthony, to obtain for me of our divine Saviour the remission of my sins, true amendment of life, consolation and help in distress, and finally the everlasting joys of heaven. Amen.

At Vespers.

I will praise Thee, O God, in St. Anthony, whose tongue never ceased to praise Thee and to incite others to praise and exalt Thee.

V. O God, incline unto my aid.

R. O Lord, make haste to help me.

Glory be to the Father, etc.

Hymn.

Now our hymn is consecrated
  To the power of thy word,
Which with marv'lous strength was
    freighted,
  Till the very beasts had heard,
Falling down, had praised their
    Maker;
  Fishes swimming close to shore;
All the earth thus made partaker
  In thy rare celestial lore.
Who is there can tell the story
  Of the wonders of his life?

Sent by God to spread His glory,
And to help us in the strife.

Antiphon. Anthony had dominion over the fishes of the sea and the beasts of the earth. He increased in grace and wisdom, and defeated the heretics.

V. May God have mercy on us through thy intercession, St. Anthony.

R. May He cause the light of His countenance to shine upon us. (Ps. lxvi.)

Prayer.

O merciful God, Thou true Light of the erring, Who didst vouchsafe to lead, through the wisdom of St. Anthony, so many thousands of souls from the darkness of sin: enlighten our hearts that they may come to the knowledge of Thy divine will and persevere in the way of Thy command-

ments. Who livest and reignest world
without end. Amen.

At Compline.

I will praise Thee, O God, in St.
Anthony, whose tongue never ceased
to praise Thee and to incite others to
praise and exalt Thee.

V. Convert us, O God, Our Saviour.

R. And turn off Thy anger from us.

V. O God, incline unto my aid.

R. O Lord, make haste to help me.

Glory be to the Father, etc.

Hymn.

Darkness falls: dear saint, we hail thee,
    Who in dying saw the Lord.
Though 'twas dark, light did not fail
        thee:
    Mary led thee up to God.
Softly death crept in and found thee,
    Stilled the longing of thy soul,

Gently loosed the cord that bound
  thee,
Led thee forward to thy goal.
Wailing, through the orphaned city
  Rose the cry: "The saint is dead!"
Thou didst comfort them: in pity
  Pray for us, to-day, instead.

Antiphon. Thou art My servant. I
have chosen thee and not cast thee
away. (Is. xli.)

V. The Lord loved him and gave
him renown.

R. He clothed him with the garment
of His glory.

Prayer.

O most merciful Jesus, Who on a
Friday didst die upon the wood of the
cross, and on a Friday, too, didst receive the pure soul of Thy faithful servant Anthony in reward of the sincere
compassion with which he contem-

plated Thy sacred Passion: graciously grant us also to meditate truly on Thy sufferings. Through them, and through the intercession of St. Anthony, lead us to eternal bliss in heaven. Where Thou livest and reignest world without end. Amen.

Conclusion.

Dearest saint, in praise unending,
    Let me thank thee for thy care.
At thy feet, thy love befriending,
    Dare I hope the Lord will spare—
For the Christ-child, who once sought
        thee,
    In thy loving arms who lay,
So much of His Heart has taught thee,
    That He cannot say thee nay.
Ah, while earth is still my dwelling,
    Every day be thou my friend;
Fill my soul with peace, foretelling
    Perfect bliss that hath no end.

LITANY OF ST. ANTHONY.

For Private Devotion.

Lord, have mercy on us.

Christ, have mercy on us.

Lord, have mercy on us.

Christ, hear us.

Christ, graciously hear us.

God the Father of heaven,

God the Son, Redeemer of the world,

God the Holy Ghost,

Holy Trinity, one God,

Have mercy on us.

Holy Mary, conceived without sin,

St. Anthony of Padua,

St. Anthony, glory of the Brothers Minor,

St. Anthony, lily of virginity,

St. Anthony, gem of poverty,

Pray for us.

St. Anthony, example of obedience,

St. Anthony, mirror of abstinence,

St. Anthony, vessel of purity,

St. Anthony, star of sanctity,

St. Anthony, model of conduct,

St. Anthony, beauty of paradise,

St. Anthony, ark of the testament,

St. Anthony, keeper of the Scriptures,

St. Anthony, teacher of truth,

St. Anthony, preacher of grace,

St. Anthony, exterminator of vices,

St. Anthony, planter of virtues,

St. Anthony, conqueror of heretics,

St. Anthony, terror of the infidels,

Pray for us.

St. Anthony, consoler of the

   afflicted,

St. Anthony, searcher of con-

   sciences,

St. Anthony, martyr in desire,

St. Anthony, terror of the devils,

St. Anthony, horror of hell,

St. Anthony, performer of mir-

   acles,

St. Anthony, finder of lost things,

St. Anthony, helper of all who in-

   voke thee,

Pray for us.

Be merciful, *spare us, O Lord.*

Be merciful, *hear us, O Lord.*

From all evil,

From all sin,

From the snares of the devil,

From pestilence, famine, and war,

From eternal death,

Through the merits of St. An-

   thony,

Through his ardent charity,

Deliver us, O Lord.

Through his zealous preaching,

Through his desire of martyrdom,

Through his strict observance of obedience, poverty, and chastity,

On the day of judgment,

We sinners, *beseech Thee, hear us.*

That Thou vouchsafe to lead us to true penitence,

That Thou vouchsafe to inflame us with divine love,

That Thou vouchsafe to let us ever enjoy the protection of St. Anthony,

That Thou vouchsafe to give us, by the merits of St. Anthony, the gift of true contrition, humility, and contemplation,

That Thou vouchsafe us the grace, through the intercession of St. Anthony, to overcome

Deliver us, O Lord.

We beseech Thee, hear us.

the world, the flesh, and the
devil,

That Thou vouchsafe the assistance of St. Anthony to all who
invoke him in their necessities,

That Thou vouchsafe graciously
to hear us,

Son of God,

We beseech Thee, hear us.

Lamb of God, Who takest away the
sins of the world, *spare us, O Lord.*

Lamb of God, Who takest away the
sins of the world, *hear us, O Lord.*

Lamb of God, Who takest away the
sins of the world, *have mercy on us.*

Christ, hear us.

Christ, graciously hear us.

V. Pray for us, O blessed Anthony.

R. That we may be made worthy of
the promises of Christ.

Let us Pray.

Almighty and eternal God, Who

didst glorify Thy faithful confessor
Anthony with the perpetual gift of
working miracles, graciously grant
that what we confidently seek through
his merits we may surely receive
through his intercession. Through
Christ Our Lord. Amen.

THE RESPONSORY TO ST. ANTHONY.

If miracles thou fain wouldst see:
Lo, error, death, calamity,
The leprous stain, the demon flies,
From beds of pain the sick arise.

The hungry seas forego their prey,
The prisoner's cruel chains give way;
While palsied limbs and chattels lost,
Both young and old recovered boast.

And perils perish; plenty's hoard
Is heaped on hunger's famished board,
Let those relate, who know it well,
Let Padua of her patron tell.

The hungry seas, etc.

Glory be to the Father, etc.

The hungry seas, etc.

V. Pray for us, blessed Anthony.

R. That we may be made worthy of the promises of Christ.

Let us Pray.

O God! Let the votive commemoration of blessed Anthony, Thy confessor, be a source of joy to Thy Church, that she may always be fortified with spiritual assistance, and may deserve to possess eternal joy. Through Christ Our Lord. Amen.

An indulgence of one hundred days each time. A plenary indulgence once a month.

O GLORIOSA DOMINA!

Hymn to the Blessed Virgin Mary, that St. Anthony was wont to repeat.

O glorious Virgin, ever blessed,
All daughters of mankind above,

Who gavest nurture from thy breast
　To God with pure maternal love.

What we have lost through sinful Eve,
　The blossom sprung from thee re-
　　stores,
And granting bliss to souls that
　grieve,
　Unbars the everlasting doors.

O gate through which hath passed the
　　King!
　O hall whence light shone through
　　the gloom!
The ransomed nations praise and sing
　The Offspring of thy virgin womb!

Praise from mankind and heaven's
　　host,
　To Jesus of a virgin sprung,
To Father and to Holy Ghost,
　Be equal glory ever sung.　Amen.

O LINGUA BENEDICTA !

When St. Bonaventure had the grave opened in which the remains of St. Anthony had reposed for thirty-two years, the tongue of the saint was found well preserved and red as in the days when he preached the word of God.

O blessed tongue! that always blessed the Lord, and made others bless and praise Him; it is now manifest what great merits thou dost possess in the sight of God.

V. Pray for us.

R. That we may be made worthy, etc.

Let us Pray.

O almighty God, Who alone dost perform miracles, grant, we beseech Thee, that, as Thou didst preserve the tongue of Thy holy confessor, St. Anthony, incorrupt after death, we, through his intercession and after his example, may be worthy of praising and blessing Thee forever.

Through Christ Our Lord. Amen.

ST. ANTHONY'S BLESSING AGAINST
THE ASSAULTS OF THE POWERS OF
HELL.

Behold the cross of the Lord! fly,
ye powers of darkness; the Lion of
the tribe of Juda, the root of David,
has conquered. Alleluia!

One hundred days' indulgence once a day.—Leo
XIII., May 21st, 1892.

THREE PRAYERS TO BE SAID KNEELING
BEFORE A PICTURE OF ST. ANTHONY
IN AFFLICTION OR ANXIETY OF ANY
KIND.

O loving Jesus, source of grace and
mercy, I cast myself at Thy feet, and I
implore Thee, through the love which
St. Anthony bore Thee, and through
the compassionate Heart with which
in Thy bitter agony Thou didst look
down upon Thy Mother from the cross
and commend her to the care of St.

John, to look upon me, a poor sinner, with the eyes of Thy boundless mercy. Come as my loving Father and God to my assistance in my great need and anxiety. In Thee do I trust, in Thee do I hope. Amen.

Our Father, Hail Mary.

O good Jesus, loving Redeemer and Sanctifier! I cast myself at Thy feet, and I implore Thee through the love which St. Anthony bore Thee, and through Thy precious blood shed for us, to turn Thy compassionate and fatherly eyes upon me, a poor sinner whom Thou didst free on the cross from the chains of the enemy. Comfort me in my anxiety and affliction, for in Thee alone do I place all my confidence and my hope. Amen.

Our Father, Hail Mary.

O loving Jesus, sure and sole refuge

of my needy soul! I cast myself at Thy
feet, and I implore Thee through the
love which St. Anthony bore Thee,
and through Thy love for him which
induced Thee to come to him in the
form of a little child, and to comfort
and caress him, I implore Thee to
come to me in my great need and
affliction, that I may know how precious is Thy presence in a soul that
hopes in Thee.

Our Father, Hail Mary.

Prayer.

O truest and most loving patron St.
Anthony! I implore thee in union with
the most loving Heart of Jesus, which
He suffered to be opened for sinners
after His death, show me how great is
thy power before the throne of God,
and let me be comforted in my afflic-

tion with the hope that, like all who call upon thee in their need, I may be able to say with a joyful heart, God truly lives and reigns in His servant St. Anthony.   Amen.

Concluding Prayer.

St. Anthony, I love thee!

St. Anthony, I praise thee!

St. Anthony, I implore thee!

St. Anthony, I hope in thee!

St. Anthony, protect me!

St. Anthony, enlighten me!

St. Anthony, strengthen me!

St. Anthony, I give myself to thee!

Forsake me not at the hour of death!

Protect me against the wicked enemy!

Defend me before the judgment seat!

Accompany me to eternal joy!

And I will praise thee forever.   Amen.

PRAYER AT THE END OF THE NINE TUESDAYS.

God be praised, through Whose grace I have carried out this devotion. Nine times, O St. Anthony, have I visited thy image with confidence to lay before thee my necessities, often have I poured forth prayers and sighs to thee, and I have striven, as far as possible, to offer thee true and faithful service in order to promote thy honor to the best of my power and manifest my sincere love for thee. If I have truly done my duty thou wilt do thine, and give me a practical proof that my devotion is pleasing to thee, and that thou art a saint rich in consolations. But do thou, O good St. Anthony, supply for what is lacking in my devotion! I will no longer be anxious or troubled; I will trust all to

God's mercy and thy advocacy. My only care shall be to keep Jesus, Mary, and thee for my friends. It is enough that Jesus knows my suffering, for He never forsakes one who loves Him. Amen.

PRINTED BY BENZIGER BROTHERS, NEW YORK